Cecil Lewis was born in Birkenhead in 1898, joined the RFC in 1916 as a pilot and was awarded the MC. After the war he went to Peking to teach the Chinese to fly. All this is recorded in *Sagittarius Rising*, recognized as a First World War classic. Returning to London he became one of the five founding members of the BBC and Chairman of the Programme Board from 1922 to 1926. He went on to write books and radio plays, directed the first two films made of Bernard Shaw's plays, was called to Hollywood where he got an Oscar for his script of *Pygmalion*, went on to beachcomb in Tahiti and returned to flying duties in the RAF in the Second World War. In 1947 flew his own aeroplane to S. Africa where he farmed sheep. Returning to New York to work for the United Nations in 1951, he was subsequently invited to join the staff of Associated Rediffusion when commercial television was set up in London a year later. He retired to Corfu in 1968. Among his other books are *Farewell to Wings*, *Never Look Back*, *Turn Right for Corfu* and *Gemini to Joburg*. At 91 he is still writing.

THE GOSPEL
ACCORDING TO JUDAS

Cecil Lewis

SPHERE BOOKS LIMITED

SPHERE BOOKS LTD

Published by the Penguin Group
27 Wrights Lane, London w8 5tz, England
Viking Penguin Inc., 40 West 23rd Street, New York, New York 10010, USA
Penguin Books Australia Ltd, Ringwood, Victoria, Australia
Penguin Books Canada Ltd, 2801 John Street, Markham, Ontario, Canada l3r 1b4
Penguin Books (NZ) Ltd, 182–190 Wairau Road, Auckland 10, New Zealand

Penguin Books Ltd, Registered Offices: Harmondsworth, Middlesex, England

First published in Great Britain by Sphere Books Ltd, 1989

Copyright © Cecil Lewis, 1989

Printed and bound in Great Britain by
Richard Clay Ltd, Bungay, Suffolk

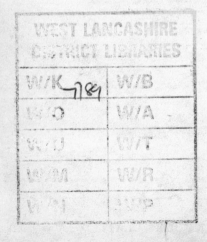

*The Author wishes
to acknowledge the inspiration of*
GURDJIEFF
in writing this book.

CHAPTER ONE

The knocking was far away. Muffled, under blankets of sleep. Knock. Knock. Knock. Nothing to do with him.

'Mr John! Mr John! Sir! Sir!'

That was Annie's voice! Annie! What was she doing . . . ?

'Sir! Mr John! Wake up! Wake up!' Damn the woman! She knew she was never to wake him . . .

Now she was rattling at the handle. Frantic.

'Mr John! For God's sake, Mr John! Mr Jude's hanged himself!'

John Colvin snapped wide awake then, called: 'Just a moment,' swung out of bed, reached for his dressing gown, knotted it round himself, and opened the door. Annie was a bundle, collapsed on the floor. Shocked. Sobbing.

'Annie! Where is he?'

'From that ring under the skylight . . . oh, sir . . . I opened the door . . . and there he was!'

John ran for the stairs. It might not be too late. The door was ajar. He pushed it wide. Jude Heddon hung there. Limp. Still. Such a look, the head cocked on one side, the long legs dangling. John heard the shouting inside his head. 'You fool! You bloody fool! Why did you have to do that?' He reached forward, touched the dangling hand. Soft. Cold. Nothing to be done . . . Suddenly he was frightened. Steady. Mustn't panic. Keep everything under control. Do what has to be done. He bent to pick up the overturned chair the dead man must have stood on and kicked away. Noted, almost subconsciously, the doubled washing line, knotted to the ring in the ceiling. You hooked the ladder into it and into the other one on the wall and climbed out onto the roof. They'd done it

together, only a few weeks back. 'Good strong hook!' Jude
had said, as he climbed. Was he thinking of it then?

He slid past the body into the living-room. He didn't want
to touch it; but he did. Set it swaying. Ought he to steady it,
stop it? Doesn't matter ... The room would be different
now. Ought to be. Must be. But it wasn't. Tidy. Ordinary.
Just as it always was. What a ghastly thing! What could have
happened? Why? He looked so thin, so helpless ... So
helpless ... John found himself staring out of the window,
seeing nothing ... The end of life! ... Useless to think about
that. Now, what to do? Must inform someone, let somebody
know. The police! Of course, the police. No near relations,
no parents, he knew that. 'You are looking at the very last
member of the Heddon line,' Jude had said, in that sardonic,
half amused, half bitter tone. 'Note the intellectual forehead,
the sensitive mouth, the effeminate hands. What a loss to
humanity!' Well, it was. Joke or not, John thought to
himself, it was. He crossed to the window. Pulled the curtain
behind the desk where the phone was.

'The Property of Mr John Colvin.' It was written in red
ink with a felt pen, scrawled across the big foolscap envelope
lying on the desk. John stared at it. *His* property! He'd no
recollection of leaving anything in the flat. He picked up the
envelope. Thick, bulging, heavy. Could it be some explanation, some confession, some reason for the thing? Maybe. But
not now ... Later. He put down the envelope, turned back
to the hall. Put out the light! Stupid to let poor Jude hang
there with that light in his eyes. Ought to cut him down
really. Couldn't leave him hanging there. But he couldn't
face that. He turned and came back to the desk, dialed 999.

They were questioning Annie. Poor Annie, all the time
smoothing her skirt across her knees and sobbing, sobbing,
until John got her to take some brandy. 'Yes, she did for Mr
Jude, once a week. Been doing for him for three years now,
come Easter. He was a good man, say what you like, a good

2

man . . . Away a lot, sometimes months, taking his pictures. Lovely pictures too, *and* he did it all himself . . . Never saw anybody in the flat, no girlfriends or anything. Pity it was, 'cos he never ate. Thin as a pin, he was. If he'd have eaten more he never would have done it, couldn't do a thing like that on a full stomach . . . Always been paid regular *and* a present when he come back from his trips. No, say what you like, he was a good man . . .' and Annie, overcome, started sobbing again . . . 'a real good man, an angel really . . .' She wiped her eyes with the back of her hand.

'Could you slip up and get my bag, Mr John?' She pulled herself together. 'I must have dropped it . . . I can't go up there again . . . Honest . . .'

The Sergeant passed her a black bag he had picked up on the landing. 'This it, Annie?'

She nodded and took it from him, got out a crumpled handkerchief, dried her eyes, blew her nose and closed the bag again. Then she sighed heavily, turning to John Colvin. 'I feel awful. Can I go now, Mr John?'

The Sergeant nodded to John and guided her to the stairs. 'Put her in a taxi, Fred,' he said to the Constable who was with him. They went down and then on the floor below, Fred's voice was heard saying to some trampling feet: 'Right at the top, mate. The Sergeant's there.'

'Must be the ambulance blokes,' the Sergeant said. 'If you'll excuse me, sir.'

'Come back if you want anything.' John closed the door. He'd better get dressed, wash and shave. Have some breakfast when they'd all gone. What a bloody business! He went into the bathroom.

A bit later there was a knock and John let the Sergeant in again. 'Sorry to trouble you again, sir . . .' They went through to the living-room. 'They've taken the body away, sir.' John nodded. It seemed indelicate to inquire where. 'Had you known him long?' the Sergeant asked, notebook in hand.

3

'About three years.'

'Then you knew him quite well?'

'Not particularly. He was just a neighbour in the top flat. He wanted a daily help. I asked Annie and she agreed to give him a morning. That's how we met.'

'She said he was away a lot.'

'Yes, abroad. He was a sort of writer/photographer. Coffee table books. Very successful. Well put together. Things about Italy, Greece, Libya.'

'Any suspicious friends dropping in and out?'

'Suspicious?'

'I'm looking for the motive, sir. People don't hang themselves without a reason. These days that could be drugs or not being able to get drugs or maybe just some of his mates rubbing out an old score . . .'

'I never heard anyone in the flat – during the daytime, that is. I work on my paper night-time, so I don't know about the evenings.'

'Would you say he was moody, depressed? Did he ever talk about doing away with himself?'

'Never. But he kept to himself. Perfectly friendly; but a bit introspective. Morbid sometimes.'

'Religious?'

'I don't know, but I think he felt guilty, in some way.'

'Guilty? What about?'

'About himself, I think, really. I always felt he blamed himself for not being better than he was.'

'Hm. Girlfriends? Boyfriends?'

'There was one girl. Liz, I think he called her. Australian. But I haven't seen her for months. I think she went back.'

The Sergeant made a note. 'Debts?'

'I wouldn't know, Sergeant; but I'd be very surprised. He didn't live it up.'

The Sergeant tapped his notebook with his pen. Then he shut it, put away the pen. 'Well, I don't see we can take it any further for the present. Thank you, sir.'

'I wish I could help more,' said John, 'but I'm as mystified as you. I s'pose we'll just have to put it down to "unsound mind" and leave it at that.'

'I suppose so, sir. But who's of sound mind now, that's what I wonder. These gangs, with their hold-ups and their muggings, have they got sound minds? And them guerrillas with their hostages and murders, I wouldn't say their minds was sound, far from it. In my job you sometimes wonder if anybody's got a sound mind!'

There was a knock on the front door. John went and found a police officer there. 'Good morning, sir. Is Sergeant Friend here?' But the Sergeant was right behind him.

'Good morning, Inspector,' he said, 'This is Mr John Colvin whose been helping us.'

The Inspector shook hands. 'Excuse me, sir,' he said, 'but I'm a bit pushed this morning. May I take Sergeant Friend right upstairs? I take it it is the top flat, Sergeant?'

The two men hurried off. 'Did you find anything?' John heard the Inspector ask. He closed the door and went in to make himself some coffee, black and strong. Ought he to have said something about the envelope? He had brought it down and put it away in his desk before the police arrived. After all it was clearly addressed to him. His property, as the writing said. It had nothing to do with the law. Or had it?

The bell rang again. It was the Inspector.

'We found this. On the mantelpiece. The late Mr Heddon's will. It wasn't sealed. Did you know he'd left everything to you, sir?'

'To me?' It made John stammer. 'To me? You must be joking.'

The officer shrugged. 'Here's the paper, sir. Not a legal will; but perfectly clear.'

'But . . . it's impossible! Here, let me see.'

The Inspector handed over the paper. It was scrawled in red ink, obviously in a hurry: 'I leave everything to my friend, John Colvin.'

5

John handed back the paper, speechless, shaking his head.

The Inspector put it back in his pocket. 'Have you a solicitor, sir?' he asked. John said that he had. 'There'll have to be inquiries. Formalities. I think you'll need his advice.' John thanked him; but he went on, 'Do you happen to know anything about his relatives, sir?'

'He had none. He told me only a few weeks ago.'

'Ah! Then, sir, as you're the sole beneficiary under the will, may we assume you'll take care of the – er – arrangements?'

John said that he would and the two officers left.

It wasn't until next morning that he got round to opening that envelope. It had kept coming up in his mind, but there had been so much to do, he hadn't even returned to the flat. The shock of the thing had gradually worn off, but all day, as he went through the tedious routine which is the paraphernalia of death, the riddle of the envelope came back. Would it offer some explanation? For there must surely be some explanation. On the surface it was all so normal: a moderately successful man, living alone, with an interesting job, at which he was quite expert. For John, thinking it over, realized how skilful he was; the photographs themselves were remarkable and it was this, combined with terse, factual information, always to the point, often amusing, sometimes containing tidbits of offbeat historical gossip, that flipped the books up out of the ordinary and made them sell. On the Continent too. Good photos were welcome anywhere and captions were no problem to translate. Then why? It was baffling. There had been hints, of course. Annie, busy with her dusting, would sometimes gossip. 'That Mr Jude don't eat nothing, Mr John. Don't get up 'til eleven most days. Lying in bed, smoking, smoking, smoking. Can't be right now, can it? Won't let me get him anything, 'cept sometimes a cup of black coffee ... And what happens the mornings I'm not there? "Not to worry, Annie dear," he says, always

6

calls me "Annie, dear," he does. I'm dreaming up a new book, he says. But 'taint right, Mr John, is it? Thin as a pin, he is. Can't come to no good, I say.'

How right she had been, John thought now, though at the time he hadn't paid much attention. As their casual acquaintance had grown a bit closer, John had built up a picture of a lonely, moody man, sometimes perfectly cheerful and good company, then suddenly plunged into black moods, introspective, revealing a guilt complex that was sometimes frightening. 'Is there any purpose in life?' he had asked John once. 'I mean, is there some standard we ought to live up to, but don't?' or another time: 'Do you ever think about sin? What does it mean "the remission of sins"?' John hadn't been able to answer. He'd just mumbled something about doing the best you can and changed the subject. He felt uncomfortable, as most men do, faced with serious subjects they don't like to think about. But when he wasn't in these black moods, he could be quite amusing, chattering about his trips, the people he had met, all the superficialities of the job, making it all sound fun and hiding the obvious flair the man must have had for picking up those nuggets of anecdote or gossip that gave his books their special flavour. But something had evidently been going on underneath . . .

When he'd returned from his last trip to Greece and Israel, he'd been in quite good form. 'I've got a winner this time, John,' he had said. 'Real humdinger.' But when John had called him a week later, he was plainly in one of his moods, monosyllabic, almost rude. The best he could manage was, 'Sorry old man. I've got problems.'

He might already have made up his mind then, John reflected. But why had he decided to leave him everything? A man he hardly knew. John shook his head. He blamed himself. Why hadn't he been more sympathetic, more intuitive? After all the Samaritans had accepted him as a more or less sensible, reliable type. It was part of his responsibility to be on the alert for things of this kind. He ought to have got the man to open up a bit, talked to him more. He might have saved him . . . a man in his forties . . . It had never even occurred to him. He expected people to phone him, pour out their troubles . . . and here, right next to him, his neighbour, a man he knew . . . A decent man, and he hadn't said a word . . . It was terrible. Ghastly . . . He still saw him hanging there . . . He would never forget it. Well, whatever he might have done, he hadn't done it. It was no good now . . .

John leaned forward and lifted the big envelope out of the bottom drawer of his desk. It was heavy. He turned it over, weighing it in his hands. *The Property of John Colvin.* Curious way to address it, as if to make sure it would reach him. What could be in it? A manuscript? Diary? Confessions? Photos? He slit open the package with his paper knife.

Inside there were papers. A single sheet on top, scrawled in red ink like the Will, read: *John. This will explain. Sorry for the trouble. Jude.*

He read the note through several times. His last words, probably. Then he put it aside. The thing looked like a diary. Carefully, neatly written. Closely spaced. A lot of words. He riffled through it. Different pens, different inks . . . There was something slightly spooky about the whole thing. Dead man's hand. A man who'd been alive yesterday . . . What had gone on? What a façade life was! You never had the least idea of what lay beneath the mask. And you couldn't find out. Death buried all secrets, except those you chose to leave behind – like these pages . . . He didn't look forward to reading them. It might involve him in all sorts of complications. He was a man who always tried to avoid complications . . . He sighed and put the bundle down on the desk. Not yet. He got up, paced up and down the room. He found he was still shaken. It all came back to him, the bulging eyes, the swaying body . . . He had failed miserably. He ought to have seen it coming. What could have been the

8

motive? Death, self-inflicted death, was a grim subject after all. And he was such a decent chap, an interesting, sensitive man, a man who somehow evoked pity, gave the impression of being lost ... That was the way he thought of him. That was the way he wanted to remember him. And now this great bundle of words might reveal crime, vice, all sorts of things he didn't want to know anything about. He stopped before the desk and looked down on the papers. Well, it was part of the legacy, after all. He'd better get on with it ... He sat down, pulled the papers towards him and began to read.

CHAPTER TWO

29.9.73. Flew in from Athens. Touch down 4.30. Very thorough baggage check. My two camera boxes carefully gone through for guns or bombs or drugs. Good thing there are full details on my passport. Tel-Aviv hot and heavy after the clarity of autumn in Greece. Representative of the tourist people met me, as arranged. Good-looking young man. Flattered me by knowing about my books – or so he said. Nice to feel like a VIP. Apparently they'd laid on quite a programme for me. The young man, David, was a bit put out when I told him it wasn't on. I tried to explain that that sort of approach was no good to me. I must browse round on my own and get the feel of a place first. I wasn't a guide book illustrator, I told him. He took it very well – 'Anything you say. We're here to help.' He asked where I was staying and when I said I'd booked in at Jerusalem and asked where I could get the bus, he insisted on driving me there himself. 'Only an hour,' he said. I told him it was quite unnecessary; but he wouldn't hear of it. 'I'd get a rocket if I didn't see you settled in.'

Tel-Aviv noisy and crowded. Too many people, cars, buses, et al, and faceless, like any other modern city. But cooler and more pleasant once we began to climb into the hills. I hadn't realized Jerusalem was 2000 ft. up. Got the young man, David, talking about himself. He'd just finished his army training – parachutist. He was married and had a young son. Very enthusiastic about Israel. No country like it to his way of thinking. I must say I did get a feeling of excitement, sort of vibration of going places. Don't quite know why. Of course their record, in such a short time, is amazing. 'These poor bloody wogs,' he said, 'what did they do for Palestine? All those centuries! Nothing! And now look at it!' I said I hoped to do just that. 'You'll see, Mr Heddon, you'll see.' He was quite worked up. 'We're making a land flowing with milk and honey.' Funny to hear the biblical phrase coming out like that . . .

David put me down at my hotel, gave me his full name and telephone number, told me where to find the Tourist office in Jerusalem and said if I wanted anything, but anything, I'd only to contact him. A very pleasant first impression.

30.9.73. Spent the morning wandering round the town. Bought a couple of shirts, drip-dry. Must change every day in this heat. Old city picturesque; but I can see if I'm going to get any shots I'll have to be up at dawn. The cars cut off the feet of the buildings, so they don't stand on anything. Just like Italy – where it was impossible.

It had never struck me before; but here's Jerusalem – which we always think of, geographically, as the very fountainhead of Christianity – and it's only a sideshow, a tourist attraction, in an absolutely Jewish city! Over the centuries the Church has fostered a hatred of the Jews and yet here we are after 2000 years still sort of second class citizens in our own Holy Places! I suppose that's what the Crusades were about. And the Arabs reckon they've a pretty good claim to it too. Wasn't Mahomet supposed to have been taken up into heaven from here? Seems a good case for internationalization. But I don't see the Jews giving it up.

1.10.73. Visited the Church of the Holy Sepulchre. Find myself very cynical about all the 'holy places'. Who knows where they really were? 'Tradition' says *this* took place here, *that* took place there; but Jerusalem has been destroyed again and again – look at the difficulty in deciding exactly where our own Elizabethan landmarks are, and they're only 500 years old. I think it's extremely unlikely that any of the chosen places are genuine. I suppose it doesn't matter, but it seems so naive, as if the whole thing were no more than a fairy tale. If people's belief was fostered by their pilgrimages – to Mecca or Lourdes – or Stratford even – it would be different. But is it? I suspect it's mostly just another trip, like visits to the Parthenon or Delphi, or the Coliseum. I am bound to say commercializing the Crucifixion revolts me. Do I really want to do a book on all this fakery? I see my father coming out in me. He was a fanatic about truth – or rather betraying the truth.

3.10.73. Took a bus down to Bethlehem. Can't get over how close all these places are. It's such a small country. Not many tourists. Too hot for them yet. Bus full of people, all very friendly and uninhibited. Mostly young. Found myself next to a young woman from Kensington! It seemed absolutely incongruous. I couldn't help laughing. She had emigrated three years ago. Her husband sold fertilizers. She enquired, a bit nostalgically I thought, about the King's Road and the Proms. 'Did I go to the Proms? Did I happen to know a young man called John Parkin who did photographs for Peter Jones?' I gathered he'd been a boyfriend of hers – long ago, it seemed. And now? 'It was wonderful here,' she said. 'A new life! Europe was finished,' she thought. 'Bogged down. Clapped out. Poor England!' 'Did she regret leaving?' I asked. 'Regret leaving!' It seemed a good joke to her. 'In London I just existed,' she said, 'here I live!' I envied her her whole-heartedness.

Bethlehem terribly depressing. The commercialism, the gift shops, the souvenirs. Picture postcards and icecream . . . What have we come to?

4.10.73. Decided to take a trip down to the Dead Sea. Don't know much about the things they've found there, but at least the excavations and scrolls can be accurately dated and one gets a feeling of it all being 'real'. Impressive drop to the place and really hot. Booked into this dreadful great barracks of a hotel in the middle of nothing. Dead Sea below. 'Dead' is the right word. I got a feeling I was really in the wilderness. Talk about the abomination of desolation, this was it. Absolutely barren. Even the water looked dead. Felt I must take a dip in it – just to say I'd done so and felt ridiculous floating half out of water, like a sea-lion, floundering . . . Sunset really impressive. Real moon landscape. Glad of the air conditioning.

After dinner I was picked up by a millionairess! American, of course. Like me she was on her own and, as I walked past her, going out, a miniature white poodle, all tarted up with shampoo and ribbons, dashed out from under her table and barked at me furiously. I stopped. I have a weakness for poodles. They're so smart, so lively.

'Topsy!' A strong, heavily jewelled hand scooped the dog up under her arm and I found myself looking into the owner's face, a smooth, rather gaunt, skilfully made-up face with tragic eyes.

'Hi!' she said. 'I guess Topsy startled you.'

I shook my head and smiled. 'I rather go for poodles.' I stretched out the back of my hand towards Topsy's muzzle and that young lady, after some hesitation, consented to sniff it disdainfully.

'You're honoured,' said her owner. 'Usually she snaps.'

'She's great,' I said.

'You alone?' Her eyes were looking me over.

'Yes.'

'Sit down. Join me for coffee.' It was almost a command. The waiter, who'd been hovering about the table, whisked out a chair and I found myself sitting with her. When you're travelling alone there's nothing much to do at meals except look at the other guests and I'd noticed the woman. She was getting a lot of attention, I thought. I tried to place her. Obviously American. Well heeled. If the clasp and the rings

13

were real, I thought, it spelt money. I heard the twang of her accent as she ordered. Across the room, the face looked strained. Near to, well, it made me nervous. Faultlessly turned out, of course, make-up, manicure, hair-do, perfect.

She held out her hand. 'My name's Caesar,' she said. 'My friends call me Julia.'

I took the hand. 'Heddon,' I said, 'Jude Heddon.'

'You here on vacation?'

I told her it was business. I took photographs and made books out of them. Watching her face as I talked somehow, I don't know why, I began to feel sorry for the woman.

'You mean you can live off that?'

'Just.'

She stared at me as if she didn't understand. 'Well, what d'you know?' was the best she could manage.

'You married?' I was being labelled. No, I told her. I lived alone. 'You don't say! That'd kill me. You mean you don't need a playmate, someone to drink with, someone for company?'

'It depends who that someone is.'

'Oh, sure, sure. It has to be right ...' She broke off, thinking, and then added with something like a sigh, 'And I never seem to get it right, I guess.' The whisky bottle was at her elbow, half empty. Now she poured herself a stiff one. 'Scotch?' She lifted the bottle towards me. I shook my head. She emptied her glass. Alcoholic? I wondered. It looked that way. Now she went back to her earlier thought '... so I just keep jogging around on the old carousel ... Waiting for death, I guess ...'

It gave me the shivers. But she pulled herself together, 'Say, why am I talking to you like this?'

I told her it was probably because she'd never seen me before and would never see me again. So she could loosen up and say anything she liked. 'That's right.' She seemed surprised. It was evidently a new thought to her. 'So I can kick off my knickers and have fun! Say, you're a nice guy . . . Whaddusay your name was?'

'Heddon, Jude Heddon,' I repeated.

'You're a nice guy, Jude.' She evidently wanted to talk about herself. 'You never heard of the Caesars, I guess?' I shook my head. 'Well, next to Fort Knox, we're it!'

'A lot of money must be a great responsibility.'

'You're damn right. Things look different when you're rich. You get so you can't trust nobody. My old Dad kept piling it up. It was fun to him. Then he found he couldn't stop it! Sort of got to have a life of its own! Kinda funny, in a way – to him, that is. But when he died and I got to handle it, that spelt trouble . . . Not at first, though. At first it was great. I was young. I could have anything I wanted. There were lots of guys around helping me spend my money. Why not? There was plenty of it. But then, it all went bad on me. I fell for a guy, really fell for him. You know, all the way . . . He was a honey, Jude, a real honey, or so I thought – then . . . Well, he taught me about love all right.' Her voice faltered and tears were near. But she snapped out of it. 'After it fell apart, I didn't care what happened. Drink, drugs, fornication, jetting all over the world . . . But I came to the end of that too after a few years. I got older, I guess. But the money was still there, and a bunch of creeps too, all telling me how to spend it, manage it, give it away. But, every so often I run out on 'em. That's why I'm here.' She paused and looked at me, ready to share a secret. 'See that little man over there?' She pointed. 'That's Father Gregory. He says he's going to save my soul and, boy –' she tried a laugh – 'does it need saving!' There was something genuine, endearing about the way she said it.

I had noticed the man she pointed out earlier. He was sitting with another man, white haired, heavy and powerful, seventy if he was a day. The two seemed to have a lot to say to one another.

'He doesn't know I'm here yet,' Julia Caesar was going on. 'I just got in before supper.'

'And how is he going to save your soul?' I asked her, a bit sceptically.

'Well, you see Jude, I was brought up Catholic and every so often, when things get bloody, I wonder if it might help. This Father Gregory wants to get me interested in things, so he got me to come down here trying to sell me the idea that I'd find all these caves and ruins and things. He said it was just what I needed . . . But it all looks a bit dried up to me.'

I thought it might help to encourage the woman – after all she sounded in a pretty bad way – so I said, cheerfully, 'Why not give it a chance? It would be something quite new for you.'

She looked at me in a curious way. I ought to have seen the signs. 'You might get a kick out of it,' I went on, 'anyway it would give the Holy Father a lift!'

A mad look came into her eyes. She glared at me. 'Why should I give him a lift?' She had raised her voice. 'Why should I give anyone a lift. Nobody ever gave me a lift. You're a bloody do-gooder, like all the rest.'

The woman was drunk. I hate scenes. So I got up abruptly. But she clutched my arm. I don't think she knew what she was saying. 'Don't go! I can't help it, kid. Honest I can't. I hate this bloody country. Can't think why I came here.'

She tried to get to her feet; but with Topsy under one arm, it was too much for her. I had to help her up.

'Thanks, kid. You're real good to me.' Clutching my arm, we made our way, rather unsteadily, towards the lifts. As we did so, Father Gregory, who had evidently seen Mrs Caesar leaving, hurried across.

'Good evening, Mrs Caesar. I'm so glad you've managed to come down.' He was all over her, much too smarmy for me. 'My uncle's with me, Dr Ramsay, back from India. We're going to have a look round the ruins in the morning.

We'd be delighted if you'd join us. I think you'll find it really interesting.' He turned to include me: 'And your friend too, of course, if he'd care to.'

'Well, I might at that,' she managed to say. 'Give me a ring in the morning, huh?'

'I will indeed,' and the Father excused himself and left.

We continued on our way, in slow motion, and got to the lifts at last. 'Thanks, kid,' she kept saying. 'You're being real kind to me, kid.' She was maudlin, tearful, pathetic – poor woman.

'Got any Valium?' I asked her.

'It's my lifeline.'

'Then take some and have a good night's sleep.'

'I will that.'

I helped the woman into the lift and left her, glad to get away.

I turned back towards the terrace to get some fresh air. The mixture of stale whisky and perfume had made me feel a bit sick. And there was something depressing too, something lost, hopeless about the woman. Money, money, money! I don't think I've ever met a wealthy man, or woman, who led a happy life. It always seems to ruin them somehow.

I passed Father Gregory and his uncle near the terrace doors. They were just ordering coffee and, as I came by, the Father turned to me very pleasantly and asked if I'd care to join them. As we found a table and sat, the younger man introduced himself as Gregory Cippico. His uncle chipped in immediately:

'*Father* Gregory Cippico! Better give him your handle, Greg. Saves complications – if it turns out he has some plot to blow up St Peters!' He gave me his hand in a very open, generous way.

'I'm Jonathan Ramsay,' he said.

'Doctor Ramsay!' Father Gregory countered, not to be outdone. 'Chair of Comparative Studies at the University of Madras.'

'Retired,' added the Doctor.

I gave them my name, told them I was a sort of writer/photographer and added I was out in Israel to gather material for a book.

'Heddon. Heddon.' Father Gregory was puzzling at the name, searching his memory. 'Did you do that book on the Loire Châteaux?' I said that I had. 'I thought I remembered it. Very good. Excellent photos and your material, in the written part was, if I may say so, well above average. Informative, unusual and witty. You evidently do your homework.'

I was flattered of course. It's gratifying to meet some stranger and find that, unexpectedly, he knows and likes your work.

'Doing the same sort of thing out here?' he inquired. I said that I hoped to. I'd only been here a few days, I told him and was just browsing around.

'Like it?' he asked.

I suppose I paused before replying; but the old Doctor was onto it at once.

'I warn you,' he put in with his wide, knowing smile, 'don't say a word against the Holy Land to Greg. He practically wrote the Old Testament. He won the Six Day War and now he just sits back and tells the Knesset what to do!'

We all laughed; but Father Gregory wasn't going to let it go.

'Pay no attention to my uncle, Mr Heddon,' he said. 'He holds the most extravagant and heretical views about everything. Wildly inaccurate and highly suspect.'

'I assure you, Mr Heddon,' the old man leaned towards me and I began to see this sort of ribbing was evidently a line of family banter they both engaged in to mask their mutual affection, 'I assure you, there is nothing exaggerated or irreverent about my attitude to religious matters. It is simply that I find it difficult to swallow the blanket dogma of

18

Catholicism.' Father Gregory was about to expostulate, but the Doctor continued: 'You evidently, as a visitor, and an intelligent man, have certain reservations about Israel. I'd be very interested to hear what they are.'

It was an invitation to start an argument and I could see the Doctor was delighted at the prospect. He settled himself in his chair with anticipation. However I assured him I had no 'reservations' about Israel. How could I have? I'd not been here a week. 'On the contrary,' I said, 'I very much admire their remarkable record. It's quite astonishing what so few people have achieved in such a short time. No,' I went on, 'it's not Israel, it's the Holy Places that worry me.'

'How do they "worry" you?' Father Gregory's voice sounded critical.

'It's just that I can't believe in them, that they were where the guides say they are. X marks the spot and all that . . .'

'But even if there is any doubt about the actual places where these events took place – which I don't for a moment admit – what does it matter?'

'It matters,' the Doctor told him, 'because it casts a shadow of doubt on the whole operation.'

'Operation!' Father Gregory bridled, 'what a word to use! Our Lord was done to death in Jerusalem in a brutal and horrible manner and triumphed over it by His Resurrection. We commemorate the tragedy of it and worship His victory at certain places tradition has made sacred to us. If those places are a hundred yards to left or right of the spot where these things actually occurred, I cannot see that it, in any way, invalidates the act of worship. We celebrate the event.'

'If it actually occurred.' The Doctor was smiling at his nephew indulgently.

'Oh come, Uncle! Surely you aren't suggesting the whole Bible story is a myth.'

'Myth is exactly the word I would use.' Now the old man was beginning to enjoy himself. 'Myths are sort of blown-up fairytales. Parables. Often full of deep meaning, but whether the stories they relate ever really happened – that is quite another matter.'

'If you are suggesting that the entire Christian religion is a fake, I really cannot argue with you.' Father Gregory fidgeted in his chair and glared at his uncle, who remained unperturbed and smiling.

At this moment the waiter appeared with our coffee and, to change the subject, Father Gregory turned to me and said he hoped I would come with them tomorrow and walk over the ruins of Qumran and see the caves. I said I was looking forward to it. Doctor Ramsay turned to me. 'You couldn't have a better guide. Greg is by way of being a bit of an archaeologist. I believe he's the Vatican's expert on the Dead Sea Scrolls.'

'I'm nothing of the kind,' Greg put in.

'Well, he reads Hebrew and has long learned discussions with the palaeontologists on dotting the Is and crossing the Ts in versions of Micah and Habbakuk.' The Doctor chuckled in his slightly patronizing manner. 'But,' he went on, 'all the same their remarkable discoveries in the caves round here, if they do nothing else, simply corroborate the truth of what I was just saying.'

The old man had a sort of bulldog quality of hanging on to the train of the argument that interested him and I must say the way Father Gregory rose to him did seem to me a bit naive. There was a sort of veiled fanaticism in the way he barked out, 'In what way?'

'Well, consider the situation. Here, so I have read, are the ruins of a religious community, very strict practising Jews, living in the wilderness, in most inhospitable and austere conditions. The scrolls that have been found, so far, give a clear picture of their way of life and it certainly isn't kindergarten stuff. They spent their days expecting the end of the world and the coming of the New Messiah. Their records run – correct me if I am wrong – from about a century before Christ to AD 68 when the whole place was wiped out by the Roman Legions. In other words they were active during the time of Jesus' teaching – and Jerusalem, where His work came to a head, was less than thirty miles away. Now, do you mean to tell me that a great religious teacher could appear next door, so to speak, and there would be no reference whatever, not a word, not a phrase, to His existence even?'

'But why should there be?' Father Gregory was up in arms; but I couldn't resist butting in:

'That's the thing that disappointed me too. When I first read about the discoveries here, I expected they'd find new evidence, new sidelights on Christianity, but . . .'

'Exactly.' The Doctor nodded agreement. 'I felt the same. There was nothing.'

'I repeat, why should there be?' Father Gregory was so upset, he actually thumped the table. 'These people at Qumran were a very special esoteric sect. Orthodox Jews; but more orthodox than the orthodox. From their point of view Jesus would have been an infidel, a heretic, a madman. What He taught would have been anathema to them. Naturally there's no reference to Him. It's impossible that there should have been. As for proof that Jesus lived and taught here, in Palestine, we have four Gospels, giving a wealth of everyday detail, what more can anyone want?'

The Doctor was warming to his subject now and, if he was riding his hobby horse, he rode it, I thought, remarkably well. 'What historians want are cross references, sidelights, as Heddon puts it, to corroborate what is, by any standards, a striking and highly dramatic episode in the history of Jewry. Well, there is no such evidence. Josephus' reference to Jesus is now generally agreed to be spurious – and was inserted, probably, at a later date, to meet this very point.'

'All this doesn't matter in the very least,' Greg bridled. He evidently didn't like his uncle's sceptical approach at all.

'Of course not,' the Doctor replied, 'but it sets off speculation. There isn't a shred of evidence, historically, that Jesus ever existed. We think of it as a world-shaking event – and so it was – but, historically, it's all on a very small scale and took place in an almost forgotten corner of the Roman Empire. There's even a legend – probably apochryphal – that when someone asked Pontius Pilate about it twenty years later, he couldn't even remember the name of the man the Jews were so eager to get rid of! There were dozens of malefactors, dozens of crucifixions. That's the situation, historically, but of course spiritually, it doesn't matter in the least, as you say. The story is simply a peg on which to hang eternal truths.'

'If the Holy Inquisition still existed, you could be burned at the stake for what you've just said.' Greg, I could see, was deeply offended and hard put to it to maintain any appearance of equanimity.

'The Bible is Holy Writ. I believe it word for word. You spin out a silly fantasy suggesting that Our Lord is no more than a fiction – no more than Don Quixote or Sherlock Holmes . . .' He was shaking with suppressed rage. 'I – I won't argue with you. It would be compounding a blasphemy.'

I could see the Doctor was quite surprised and upset, almost bewildered, that what he had said should be thought so offensive. But arguments about religion usually end up badly. Now his voice was warm and almost apologetic.

'Greg, don't be offended. I assure you I have the deepest respect for your belief. My apparent irreverence is only, so to speak, marginal – like a somewhat impertinent mouse nibbling at the edge of a large and very succulent cheese.'

The simile didn't appear to be particularly apt, but I laughed and Greg managed a smile.

'I don't know that likening Christianity to good cheese is much better than all the rest of the nonsense you've been talking, but never mind . . .'

Doctor Ramsay turned to me. 'You see,' he said, 'we're almost strangers. Greg and I haven't met for twenty years.

I've spent most of my life in the East, so he's not used to my approach. I believe the astringent qualities of scepticism are often useful in discussion, so I take that line and all the things that have been going round in my head for years just tumble out. I've not offended you too, I hope?'

I assured him he had not, but I excused myself, got up, said goodnight and came up to my room. Now, after writing all this up, it's past midnight. Two interesting people – and one nutty woman – in one day! My best day in Israel so far. Doc Ramsay has a splendid leonine head and unusual mixture of physical weight and mental agility. And Father Gregory? He appears sophisticated, a man of the world, but I seem to smell something naive underneath. And a bit fanatical.

CHAPTER THREE

5.10.73. Found the old Doctor having breakfast on the terrace. Joined him at his request. He inquired how I felt in the morning and I told him it was my best time. 'Same here. Same here,' he nodded. 'Lost my wife because she couldn't get up in the morning and I couldn't stay up at night. Not her fault poor woman. Funny thing, metabolism.'

I said he had mentioned living in the East last night and I asked him where. 'China and India,' he answered at once. 'China mostly. Peking, in my twenties. That's over fifty years ago now. Wonderful place – then.'

'And now?' I asked him.

'I've no idea. Many years since I was there. It must be greatly changed.'

He poured himself another cup of coffee and I found myself admiring his head. There was something noble about the way it was set on his shoulders. Clean shaven, healthy complexion, bright eyes under heavy bushy eyebrows, black under his white hair. Running to weight now; but powerful, he must have been a fine looking man in his youth. Still was, really. He gave the impression of enjoying things. His sudden exuberant gestures. He evidently liked throwing ideas into the air, the more outrageous the better, just to see if anyone would catch them.

'Did you know China had an Emperor in the twenties? Nice boy. In his teens. There wasn't much in the way of a government in North China in those days. War Lords took it in turns. Kept the boy shut away in the north end of the Forbidden City. No power. No position. No hope of his actually ruling of course; but they didn't feel quite up to, ah, bumping him off. Kept him in cold storage, so to speak. Gave him an English tutor. Nice man. I knew him slightly.'

I told him how everything I'd read about China fascinated me and how I regretted not having seen it in the old days. He nodded in a understanding way. 'It was like living in the Middle Ages. Feudal. There was no racism then. Nobody stirring up anger, hatred. They looked on the foreigner as a curiosity, indulgently, in spite of the Boxer uprising. They were a kind people . . .' He sighed suddenly, surprising me. 'A man sees his youth through a mist of emotions he can no longer feel. A few things stick up through the mist. Often quite trivial, unimportant. Yet afterwards they seem marvellous, full of meaning, full of beauty . . . Strange!'

It was strange, I thought, sitting at breakfast overlooking the Dead Sea and feeling transported into a sort of oriental twilight by this old man whom I hadn't met twenty-four hours ago! He was staring into the distance with a fixed expression, seeing something remote, romantic, materializing, as it were, out of the distant past.

'I remember. Ah, there's Greg.' He broke off, sadly.

I turned to see Father Gregory putting down the phone at the reception desk beyond the lounge.

'How does he feel in the mornings?'

'Terrible. Just like my good wife or ex-wife rather. She had a brother – it's an Italian family – who, with suitable help, produced dear Gregory. Not my nephew, really, but Luigi – that's Greg's father – married an English wife. Hence the boy's good English.'

I suppose, at his age, the Doctor was entitled to call a man going on for fifty 'boy'; but it sounded strange and I smiled. The Doctor gulped his coffee and went on. 'Jesuit trained. All the best brains in the Church are Jesuits, so I'm told. Back room boy at the Vatican, or something of the kind, I believe. But a bit of a fanatic – easy to get a rise out of him!'

'You enjoy that?'

'I suppose I do – in a way. Faith narrows a man. Puts

blinkers on him. Sees everything through a sort of holy porthole. When you've kicked about abroad, like me, seen people just as serious, just as dedicated, about quite different beliefs, it's difficult to see how men can get involved like that . . . but there it is . . . I admire his singleness of purpose, in a way. Wish I had it . . .'

Father Gregory came over. 'Morning, Uncle Jon. Morning Mr Heddon. I've just phoned Julia Caesar . . .'

'Julius Caesar!' The Doctor was astonished. 'Surely that's not possible!'

'Julia,' Greg corrected. Doc Ramsay exploded with laughter.

'Is that what the woman's called?'

'Her father must have had a sense of humour, I think,' Greg went on. 'She can't come with us. She asks if she can join us for lunch.'

'What do you want out of her?' the old man asked, mischievously.

'If she could be persuaded to finance a little project of mine,' said Father Gregory suavely, 'it would be a – er – help.'

'Just a couple of million?'

'Not quite that. But anyway, she can afford it.'

'Trust a Catholic to keep an eye on the main chance!'

Father Gregory looked at him quite steadily. 'Why not? The Church is a very large and complex organization. It has to be financed. Now, Uncle Jon, don't start an argument with me so early in the morning. Shall we go? I've brought the car round.'

We drove North along the coast of the Dead Sea for about five miles and then turned off to the left on a track over the salty flats and up onto a sort of shelf beyond which the cliffs rose pretty well sheer. This was the place called the Khirbet Qumran. It was absolutely stark, dry, barren country. Only the hardiest straggling bushes pushed through the stones where it hardly ever rained. I wondered how the Bedouin

26

and their flocks managed to survive in such a wilderness. Father Gregory pulled up near a paybox where I could see the beginnings of a narrow track leading up into the cliffs. Doctor Ramsay surveyed it all with no enthusiasm.

'You don't expect me to climb up there – in this heat?'

'It's not far – and not very steep.'

'When I get there what do I see?'

'The famous cave.'

'I've seen plenty of caves.'

'But in this one a text of Isaiah was found a thousand years older than any text previously known.'

'So?'

'So the place is historic. Sacred, in a way.'

'Well, it isn't sacred to me. I'm sorry. Take Heddon up there. I'll wait in the car.'

Father Gregory was evidently disappointed, but he turned to me politely. 'Would you care to come?'

I said that I would and got out of the car. Father Gregory did the same.

'Sure you won't come, Uncle? It really isn't far.'

'When you get to my age, you'll know what happens to old men's knees.'

Father Gregory smiled. 'You'll be all right here, then?'

'Quite all right. Glad to get rid of you. Give me time for a little meditation.'

He closed the door, we waved and started up the track.

'Does he meditate?' I asked Greg, as I followed him.

'I shouldn't be surprised. Wonderful old boy, isn't he? He's enjoyed a fascinating life and likes to talk about it. He sometimes comes up with the most unexpected things. Get him to tell you how he was once hailed as a prophet in some Indian village because he happened to be born on the seventh hour of the seventh day of the seventh month. Fabulous.'

We lapsed into silence for the path was getting steep and the going rough. Soon I was sweating freely. The heat was really something and the air oppressive. But we were, after all, 1000 feet above sea level. My cameras felt heavy and I was too preoccupied to look about me, concentrating on the stones on the track and picking places to put my feet. It didn't seem to worry Father Gregory. He was a wiry little man and, I suppose, knowing the way, it seemed easier and shorter to him. I was breathing heavily and was glad when he stopped, some yards ahead of me, turning back.

'Not far now,' he said, pointing up, 'behind that pinnacle of rock.'

I stopped and looked up. It really was a desolation. Nothing but rocks, ravines, steep screes of shale, all eroded, crumbled into a thousand gulleys and crevices, by ten thousand years of wind and sun. It was a sort of burnt out valhalla. Only when you looked back over the sea did it have a sort of forbidding grandeur.

'Thousands of caves in these cliffs.' Father Gregory pointed to dark holes here and there in the sheer faces of the rocks. 'Extraordinary that they dropped on this one!'

'D'you often come up here?' I asked him, panting up level with where he stood.

'When I can. Fascinating place when you get to know it – and when you think what's come out of it. I've been in many of the caves; but there are hundreds more. Any one of them might contain something – even today.'

'How did they happen to drop on this one?'

Father Gregory turned and continued on up the path. I followed. 'Pure luck. A kid called Mahommed was minding his goats in the usual Bedouin way – quite biblical – and lost one. He came clambering up this way looking for it. He happened to stop and look round and saw a hole in the face of the rock, so he started chucking stones to see if he could get one in. When he did so and listened to hear it fall, it didn't make a thud, but a sharp clink. He wondered what it had hit. The Bedu are always hoping to find treasure, gold, riches, Aladdin's cave and all that, so he managed to pull himself up to the hole and peered in. All he saw were some large jars. They scared him out of his wits. You see the Arabs believe that *djinni* make their homes in jars in deserted caves like these. So he forgot the goat and dashed off.'

We came round the corner and there ahead was a narrow opening. It lay under a sort of fault and you could easily have passed it but for the way the entrance had been broadened and smoothed out by the hundreds of visitors that had climbed up to see it.

'There's the hole! There!' Father Gregory was pointing to a hole just about big enough to crawl through to the left of the opening. 'The entrance was made later when they came back and started to loot the place.'

He went ahead into the cave and I squeezed through after him, glad to be out of the glare of the sun. It was narrow, the sides curving to meet overhead and the floor thick soft dust. I began to get that slightly uneasy claustrophobic feeling I always get in underground places, the idea that the rock might fall on you at any moment. But Father Gregory was obviously in his element.

'I must say I wish I'd been that lad! To have looked in and seen those jars for the first time – untouched, hidden for almost two thousand years!'

I couldn't raise any enthusiasm for it whatever. Funny. I make my living out of photographing the romantic past; but this place was so absolutely unromantic it left me cold. 'When they got inside the cave later,' he went on, 'they found some bundles of cloth in one or two of the jars. They were hoping for gold, jewels – or silver coins anyway. These bundles of rags looked useless and even the rolls of brown leather they found inside covered with writing meant nothing at all to them.'

'They'd no idea what they'd got?'

'Absolutely no idea at all. It's quite fantastic. However they took them down to their tents, Everybody had a look at them and they decided to carry them around a bit in case they could find some use for them. A few weeks later they went into Bethlehem and showed them to a friend of theirs, a cobbler. He thought he might be able to use the leather. They kicked about on the floor of his shop for some weeks – imagine! A complete text of Isaiah! As clear and legible as if it had been written yesterday!'

'To an expert.'

'No. To anyone. Anyone who reads Hebrew. That's another extraordinary thing. The script hasn't appreciably changed in two thousand years.'

'When did they tumble to the fact that they were onto a goldmine?'

'Not for some time. The cobbler, a chap called Kando, took one scroll up to Jerusalem. He didn't know what it was; but he had a hunch it might be old. So he showed it to the Metropolitan at the Syrian Convent of St Marks, where he left it on a security of £25!'

'Twenty five pounds!'

'It seems impossible now; but then, at the start, nobody could believe it. Such things, two thousand years old, couldn't exist. However, finally the American School of Oriental Studies tumbled to it. Then the search was on. The cliffs all round here were combed for caves.'

'Did they find a lot?'

'Oh, yes. Hundreds of scrolls – or bits of them. Soon the going price was a pound a square centimetre and went on rising.'

'Have they cleaned the whole place out now?'

'One never knows. There's been nothing for some years. The Bedouin – they brought in most of the scrolls – are pretty thorough when there's money in it – and particularly big money.'

'What's the price now?'

'Depends on the scroll and the condition it's in. Anything in good shape would be practically priceless.'

Clearly this was a story that would have to go into my

book. It was just as important as the so-called 'holy places', part of the history of Jewry, and of course a tourism high spot too; but curiously it didn't turn me on at all. I wasn't hooked on it like Father Gregory. I said I would like to get some shots and went out into the sun.

The utter desolation of the cliffs with the Dead Sea as a backdrop was quite photographic and I covered it pretty thoroughly. Then we started down. I hadn't got the right shoes and that made it worse than going up. The loose stones slid under my feet. I didn't want to fall with my cameras. Father Gregory was very considerate and took all the care of me he could, helped me at the steep places and stopped every time I wanted to or if we found a bit of shade. To be polite I thanked him for bringing me up to see the place. 'Now I understand what the Bible means when it speaks of a wilderness,' I said.

'Yes. And one begins to realize how tough these people must have been to live in a place like this sooner than submit to what they considered to be the desecration of the Temple and the strictly religious beliefs they held. I often think we can't have the least idea of the strength of their fanaticism, their faith. Life, as we know it: ease, comfort, enjoyment, wealth – all that had absolutely no value in their eyes. They lived to preserve the purity of the Law. Nothing else mattered.'

Father Gregory saw the Doctor below and went ahead of me. 'We must get down to the car before Uncle melts!'

Below I could see the outline of some walls and Doctor Ramsay's portly figure looking forlorn at the top of some steps. I was heartily glad when we reached level ground.

'What a God-forsaken spot!' the Doctor observed when at last we reached him.

'It certainly wasn't that to the people who lived here,' Father Gregory reminded him. 'To them it was hallowed ground.'

'Well, it isn't hallowed now.' The Doctor stabbed at a

stone with the end of his stick. The heat had evidently made him short-tempered.

'I wonder!' Father Gregory evidently got a real kick from the place. 'Something remains perhaps. Here there was nothing. No hypocrisy, no lying, no greed, no temptation. Nothing but emptiness and the service of God.'

'Very impressive – if it's true.' I liked the Doctor's scepticism. 'How many people lived here?' he asked.

'A hundred. A hundred and fifty maybe. We don't know exactly. Quite a community though. Look!' And Father Gregory began to point out the plan of the place, the refectory, the kitchens, the water cisterns, the lavatories. To him it was all quite clear; but I saw nothing but a maze of stunted walls, crumbling in the barren ground. Meaningless, depressing and very hot.

'Where did they sleep?' The Doctor was quizzing him.

'Nobody quite knows. Not inside probably. Huts outside perhaps. Caves. It's an open question.'

'No married quarters?'

Father Gregory hesitated. 'There were women certainly. The place wasn't for men only. Women were admitted. Weaving, cooking, cleaning up, and so on. They seem to have been pretty well self-sufficient. They had their own kiln, for instance. The scroll jars were made here. They must have grown their own food – not much of it, I think. Scribes copied the Holy Books – they've even found the ink pots! Probably made them for the use of other places of the same kind. There seems to have been quite a lot of movement. This place was probably loosely connected with the Essenes, who are known to have had urban communities. They seem to have lived in fear of being overrun – which they finally were. But they had plenty of guts. They held firmly to their beliefs and observed the rules of their Order.'

'Oh!' The Doctor cut in at once. 'There were rules were there?'

'Very strict rules. Written down. We have them.'

'That settles it. The place couldn't have been any good.' The Doctor turned away.

'Uncle! Really!' Father Gregory's tone was condescending. 'All temporal, as well as spiritual orders, have rules. You can't have life without law.'

'Laws are obsolete before the ink is dry on the paper. They attempt to crystallize things, finalize them, as if Life stood still. It doesn't. Everything is in flux. Life is a dance. You have to have rhythm. You have to have the right attitude to things. People with the right attitude dance. They don't need rules.'

It was ridiculous, I thought, to hear them caught up in their abstruse questions and arguments. There they were, both of them, standing in the wilderness, sweating in the heat, deep in metaphysical questions which seemed to me absolutely irrelevant. I went off to try and get some shots. Then I went back to the car and waited for them to join me.

CHAPTER FOUR

8.10.73. Back home again in dear old London, thank God! War! What a business! I thought I'd never get away. Tel-Aviv airport closed. Hundreds of people stranded, held up, sleeping on sofas and chairs, walking about, waiting, waiting, waiting. Everyone glued to the radio and the whole country seething with action, like an ant's nest when you've kicked the top off. Egypt streaming over the canal. Couldn't believe the Israelis would let themselves get caught like that. Psychologically it was clever to attack on Yom Kippur – like Christmas Day with us. I heard that when immediate total mobilization was ordered, some people wouldn't forego their devotions on the Holy Day and that was why it took so long to put in any counter attack. Now it looks as if they're holding it. Wonder how it will go . . .

I think I'm an unlucky man. Things never seem to turn out quite right. I get by. My work's all right. But I want more than this. Pride, I suppose. I'd like to leave at least one really good book. Something people could refer back to centuries ahead and say: This is how it was, then. Couldn't expect the Israeli book to be that; but, all the same, maddening to have it all chopped off, frustrated by this stupid war which obviously can't solve anything . . .

Actually, I suppose, if I'd realized what was happening, those last days in Israel would have been exciting – unusual anyway. Everybody else, even the Doctor, was quite worked up. But, somehow, I felt detached all the time, like a spectator. I didn't care. Anyway the war swamped everything. There was nothing to do but get out. My whole trip wasted.

Don't suppose it'll settle down for months. Not much point in going back anyway, the moment's gone.

UK depressing. Strikes, deficits, bombs – the lot. Feel flat. Reaction I suppose. Annie fussing over me, as usual. Felt badly I hadn't got her her usual present; but I forgot. John Colvin dropped in to welcome me back, full of the war. Wanted me to give an eye-witness account for his paper; but I just couldn't. Felt quite whacked. Better after a good night's sleep . . . I hope!

9.10.73. Thought if I didn't get the sequence of the last few days down, I'd forget how it went. Might be interesting later. When I write my autobiog! So sat for an hour, mulling it over. Wish I could catch atmosphere, mood, like a real writer! But I can't, so must stick to plain narrative.

We got back from the Qumran place hot and dusty. I went up and took a shower, lay on my bed and thought. It was just as Doc Ramsay had said to Father Gregory coming back in the car. 'They haven't found anything, Greg, that's of any value whatever – except to the experts.' That was it: that was why I couldn't raise any interest in the whole thing. Of course Father Gregory insisted that the finds had basically altered our thinking about the Old Testament, the extraordinary fidelity of the narrative after two thousand years and so on; but the Doctor would have none of it. 'Listen, Greg. If there'd been ten words about the Crucifixion. A fresh slant on Caiaphas. One authentic new quote from Jesus, the whole Christian world would have been aroused. But there isn't. It may be a palaeontologist's paradise; but to me it's much ado about nothing.' Father Gregory repeated that such a thing couldn't possibly have happened. The Qumran sect had no interest whatever in current events. They lived to transmit the tablets of the Law and dreamed of the end of the world.

'They were pretty rudely jolted out of that one, anyway!' the Doctor reminded him. 'Extraordinary how dreams can acquire such substance,' he went on, 'such power, that they seem as solid and convincing as reality! But one day you have to wake up.' So it had gone on all the way home. Though I couldn't have argued it, I agreed with the Doctor. I hadn't read up on it; but, as far as I could make out, it was all Old Testament stuff. Jewish really. I wasn't a Jew. I was a Christian – or that was my label, anyway . . .

Came down just before lunch and found Mrs Caesar. Joined her for a drink. Must say she looked a different woman this morning. Years younger. Very well dressed. Elegant, in a way. She must have been pretty high the night before.

'Hi! Jude,' she greeted me. 'Sweet of you to ask me to lunch.'

I was taken aback. I said that I hadn't and she looked surprised. 'But you rang me this morning.' Again I said that I hadn't; but of course, if she'd care to join me . . . But she was going on. 'Say, must have been that old bore Father Gregory! I was asleep when the phone rang. Could have sworn it was you. Wishful thinking, I guess!' She gave me a look; but I didn't cotton on at the time. We all like to be liked. I suppose I was vaguely flattered. 'Listen,' she went on, 'why don't we hire a cab after lunch and get out of this dump? I want to see Jericho. Y'know, "where the walls came tumblin' down" like it says in the song.' I laughed and said I'd be glad to. Just then Father Gregory and the Doctor appeared and the three of them went off together. Julia gave me a knowing wink as she left.

As soon as we were settled in the cab and driving up out of the heat, she seemed to relax. 'Jesus,' she said, 'it's good to get away.' She turned to me, very friendly. 'What I like about you, Jude,' she said, 'is you don't want anything.' I told her not to be too sure. Maybe there were lots of things I wanted. 'Well, you play it pretty cool,' and she laid a hand on my thigh. But then – I might have known it – the driver butted in. 'Pardon me, Ma'am,' he said, 'but I guess you're from little ole New York.' And from that moment he took over. We had to hear exactly why he'd emigrated and when, how long he'd been in Israel, how his wife liked it, all about his kids. It went on and on. When we got to Jericho, he turned guide and insisted on showing us everything, where those famous walls had fallen down, the actual place where Joshua had blown his trumpet and all that. This was the place where the Rift Valley started and it sure must have been an earthquake, he guessed. It drove me mad. I hate guides. I can't stand being 'shown' things. I like to see for myself. But it didn't seem to worry Julia in the least. She took it all in her stride. She had an inexhaustible stock of 'No Kidding's' and 'What do you know's'. By the time we got back, the two of them were as thick as thieves. 'So long, Julia,' was his parting shot, 'been a pleasure. I'll call round in the morning in case you need me again, okay?'

She thanked him with such a genuine air of cordiality that it quite took me in. But as soon as we were out of earshot 'Poor bastard,' she said, 'he's lonesome, I guess. All those yids go crazy to make it back to their goddam holy land and when they do, all they want is Brooklyn.'

On the pretext of saying she wanted my advice on something important, she got me to go up to her room. I was a fool to go. As soon as we were inside she said she'd been wanting to talk to me all afternoon, went straight over and poured herself a stiff whisky – and one for me. 'Listen Jude,' she said, as she fixed the drinks, 'what d'you feel about this guy Father Gregory? Is he on the level?' She brought me my drink, talking all the time. I said I knew nothing about him. I'd only met him yesterday.

'He's certainly got a great line of chat,' she said. Then, in the most casual way, as we were talking, she began to strip. I tried to take no notice.

'He wanted money, I suppose?' I said.

'Like I told you. They all do.' She had taken off her top and now kicked off her trousers and stood in nothing but briefs and a bra. 'That's better!' she said. I'm sure she

37

wanted me to see her figure, which was quite good considering her age; but she had the tact not to parade it in any way and just reached into the wardrobe for a dressing gown and slipped it on. 'Mind you,' she was going on, 'I don't say the guy's crooked. All this digging, maybe it pays off, maybe it's a good thing. After all they found Troy, didn't they? But it doesn't do anything for me.'

'Did you tell him so?'

'Sure I told him. Hanging around watching Arabs digging up a bunch of old jamjars – forget it.' She finished her drink.

'I quite agree.'

'You're a nice guy, Jude,' she said and, just as casually as she had undressed, sat down on my knee, 'And you don't want a thing, huh?' she smiled, fixing my hair in an off-hand sort of way.

I know it sounds prudish, but I was really shocked. Scared too, I suppose, in a way. I'd never met a woman who behaved like this. I didn't really know what to do. How was I going to get her off me?

'Not a thing.' I suppose I said it a bit nervously. 'I'm quite all right as I am.'

'So am I,' was all she said, settling her buttocks more comfortably on my knees. She reached across me for my glass on the table and finished it off.

I remember a man once told me that a woman's face goes off long before her body. Julia's body was ten, fifteen years younger than her face. It was trim and I suppose some men would have found it sexy; but her face, near now, far too near, with her breath, her make-up, her perfume, it was awful ... I know I'm what people call undersexed – if that means that few women excite me. Certainly this one left me absolutely cold. She leaned across me to put her glass down, rubbing her breast across my chest as she did so. I suppose it excited her.

'Aw, c'm on, Jude!' she coaxed, 'show me what you can do.'

All I wanted was to get away. 'Get me another drink, then,' I said. 'You've had mine.'

The ruse worked. Obediently she got up and went over to the tray. I got up too. Her back was towards me.

'I'm awfully sorry,' I said, as gently as I could, 'but I must go now.'

There was a moment's pause. Then she whirled round on me and if her face had been repellent before, now, in her fury, it was ghastly. 'You goddam queer!' she shouted the words at me. 'Get your fat ass out of here!' and she threw the drink in my face. I suppose I must have looked pretty silly with the stuff pouring down, drenching my shirt. It was in my eyes too and I got out a handkerchief to wipe the worst of it away. But by now she was trying to help me, rubbing me with a towel and all the time moaning, 'Jude, Jude, I'm sorry. Really I am. I know I'm a bitch, God help me. I'm sorry, kid, real sorry . . .'

By now she was sobbing; but I managed to get the towel and her hands away from me and, holding her wrists, sat her down on the bed. 'I'm sorry, kid, really I am, real sorry . . .' she was mumbling on.

What could I say? I walked towards the door. She threw herself down on the bed, sobbing into the pillows. 'Christ!' She sounded in real agony. Suddenly I felt sorry for her. But what could I do? I went out quietly and shut the door.

Writing about it now, back here in London, I see that the poor woman was just man crazy and horribly insulted when I turned her down. But at the time it upset me dreadfully, frightened me really. My own experience with Liz had been so different, so delicate, quiet, just discovering something wonderful together, but this . . . well, it gave me the creeps really.

Anyhow I got back to my room, washed the whisky out of my hair, changed my shirt, showered and put on clean clothes. I felt quite exhausted and lay down and slept. When

I woke it was dark. Eight o'clock. I felt hungry, dressed and went down to supper. I'd worked out how I'd get past her table, pretending to be interested in something else; but she wasn't there and I saw the Doctor, dining alone at the far end of the room. He waved to me.

'Why don't you join me? Greg's taken Mrs Caesar to Jerusalem.'

He inquired how I had passed the afternoon and I told him I'd been hijacked by Mrs Caesar and carted off to Jericho. He laughed. 'A somewhat overpowering woman. Used to getting her own way. But it doesn't seem to faze Greg in the least. Extraordinary organization the Catholic Church.' I asked him why, particularly.

'Because it's so tolerant, so subtle. Take Greg, for instance. He hasn't got a parish as far as I know. I've no idea what he does. We met here because it was a convenient stop off for me and he had to come here, so he said ... I sometimes think Rome runs its own private intelligence agency, used to, in the old days ... But anyway, it's no business of mine.'

I asked him if he thought Father Gregory had had any luck with Mrs Caesar at lunch.

'I didn't think so. But you never know. He talked about archaeology most of the time; but what interest that could possibly have for her, beats me! I don't think she's an easy one. No taste, no background at all. But, maybe Greg has a scheme to get her into the headlines, posing as Lady Bountiful. That might attract her.'

I remembered the tortured sobbing figure on the bed. Lady Bountiful! To change the subject, I asked where he had been. 'Down to Masada,' he replied. 'I find Israel fascinating, don't you?'

I told him, so far, no, there was nothing sympathetic about it like, say, Greece. The mixture of go-getting commercialism and violent patriotism, plus a lot of deeply ingrained religious rituals, I couldn't put them together. They didn't seem to fit.

'But that's Jewry!' he laughed. 'That's what's so fascinating. Praise God and pass the ammunition! Fanaticism, that's what it is! Not an attribute welcomed by society! But always there, mind, always there. The Crusaders were fanatics. Hitler was a fanatic. The hijackers are fanatics. If we approve their ideals, they're heroes: if we don't they're murderers! We must have scapegoats, somebody to fasten the blame on, an effigy to burn. Take these people at Qumran. Absolute fanatics. Mad. With their "sons of light" and their "wicked priest" and their vision of a sort of holy utopia – coming next week, as the movie advertisements say. Nectar. Ambrosia. Absolute, unadulterated, pie-in-the-sky! Fanatics!'

His vivacity was infectious and we laughed. He was a very good talker and I began to feel better and enjoy myself. I felt safe in such a situation. Thinking it over now, I suppose it's emotion, violence that makes me shrink back into myself. So I told him I hated fanatics; but I could see he was right.

He beamed on me. 'You see, Jude – may I call you that?' I nodded and he went on, 'suggestibility is an enormous force. If you can make your particular fanaticism persuasive enough, plausible enough, convincing enough, a lot of people will believe you – whether it's that the earth is the centre of the universe, or that the world is flat, or that all men are equal – pretty well anything you like. Once you can get the idea accepted you're off. Because, on the whole, people want to be told what to believe, how to live. Put that in doubt and you're in for trouble. The Jews murdered Jesus, after all, for just that reason.'

'Because he was a reactionary?'

'Yes. He seemed to them just a dangerous eccentric, a sort of fanatical hippie, suggesting that people should live quite another kind of life – and that, to the Jews, meant he was against the establishment, a trouble-maker, a nuisance to be got rid of. You can't put him in the same class as Newton or Einstein. Their truths can be proved. Christ's truths can't be proved in the same way. They're in a different category, in

41

the psychological, not the scientific domain. Laws, but a different category of laws.'

'Too new, you mean?'

'Yes, exactly ... You see, it seems to me that if there is any progress in life, generally – and today it's pretty easy to doubt it – it lies in the struggle to accept a reality beyond us. This is what all the great innovators do, what Jesus did, what the Buddha did. It's like a submarine current under a rough sea. To my mind it's the only hopeful sign in our turbulent world. The waves are against us, as Churchill said, but the tide is for us. Shall we go outside and have coffee?'

We found a quiet table, ordered coffee and the old man settled himself into his seat with evident satisfaction.

'Ah!' he said. 'Nothing so pleasant as to sit and talk in the evening. Conversation's about the only thing left to old men – and there isn't much of that! Tell me, do you find Greg an interesting man?'

I told him I had practically no experience of religious men at close quarters. I somehow associated them with church and preaching. When they had other interests, worldly interests as he evidently had, I couldn't quite make it fit; but he was obviously intelligent and well informed.

'He believes. That's the interesting thing about him. He really believes – and anything that contradicts or undermines what he believes is dangerous, subversive. I think he would go to some lengths to suppress any kind of speculative thought.' The Doctor turned to me, as if he were seeing me for the first time, and inquired seriously: 'Are you a Christian?'

I hesitated. I'd never faced the question head on, as it were. 'I don't know,' I said. I felt I wanted to evade the question. 'I was brought up in the Christian tradition. I don't think I could take it much further than that.'

The Doctor nodded. 'Yes. I agree. One doesn't really ask oneself these questions. I must say I have great difficulty with it. I suppose it's having a workaday mind.'

'You mean you have doubts?' I asked.

'Yes. I find I can't swallow it whole, if you see what I mean. I have no difficulty with the doctrine – the function of Jesus as Teacher; the idea that like all great religious teachers, He was sent, or appeared, or had a job to do – revitalizing mankind. I find no difficulty in any of that. But when it comes to the man, the personality, the actual life – then I do have difficulty.'

I didn't really understand. I'd always thought of the life as being the teaching. 'In what way?' I asked him.

'Well, take the Virgin Birth. Do you believe it? Can you believe it? Practically. It opens His life with a miracle that denies the whole basis of humanity. If Jesus was a MAN and came to struggle and suffer with men, then why is He born as somebody supernatural – a "holy thing", as it is said in the Annunciation. It gives us all an impossible handicap. If He was a man then He must be born as a man. If not, then of course anything can be invented. But you can't have it both ways.'

All this was absolutely new to me and I told him so. I'd always taken the Nativity as a very touching sort of fairy story.

'Everyone does. Deeply touching and moving. It evokes love and tenderness towards the Holy Child from all of us – and that's perhaps just what it's intended to do. But the Virgin Birth raises the whole question of Jesus as a real man, a genuine human being, who really existed – and Greg would have me burned at the stake for even daring to whisper the suggestion that He was a mythical fictional creation – so I have to keep my mouth shut!'

We both laughed. 'But has anybody seriously put forward such an idea?' I asked. I just couldn't believe it.

'Certainly they have. The heretical view is that a very high level, hidden school existed whose teacher posed the question: 'Suppose we wanted to portray a perfect human life and, through its suffering, give a new spiritual impulse to

43

mankind, how would we set about it?' Then, perhaps over many years, they gradually built up this wonderful compelling story, skilfully combining the maximum of human appeal with the deepest spiritual truths. Then, when it was complete, so the story goes, their Teacher suddenly died and His four closest pupils, fearing that all their work, which had become their hope, their faith, would be lost, set down all they could remember of the story. Hence the variations in the Gospels . . .' He paused. 'Of course it's a pure hypothesis, of no interest whatever except to speculative people like me.'

'Interesting, but it doesn't affect the Teaching.' I was defensive. I didn't want my childhood touched.

'Not in the least. It's just that people get the Teaching and the Life muddled up. Both the beginning and the end of Jesus' life overstep the boundaries of humanity. After all it's a basic fact that when a man dies he cannot possibly come back to life. When this happens it is a miracle – that is the laws of a higher world at work in this one. For some this increases faith; for others it is a stumbling block, magic, a sort of trick – and that decreases it. It can even cast a doubt on Christianity itself.'

The old man had been talking into the air, as philosophers often do. But now he turned to me with an alert, almost schoolboy expression of a man about to reveal a great secret.

'But that's not to say there aren't resurrections – of another kind. In fact –' and his eyes shone with an amused expression, as if he didn't expect me to believe him, 'in fact – I have seen a resurrection.'

I'd really had about enough of this religious talk; but his last remark was so unexpected, it snapped me back to attention. How could anyone have seen such a thing?

'It happened in China when I was a young man.' He paused as if weighing in his mind whether to go on or not. 'I'm not sure I ought to have seen it really . . .' He was silent again, sighed deeply at some secret train of thought, and then said, almost diffidently, 'Would you care for me to tell you about it? It isn't something I often speak about in the ordinary way.'

I couldn't help being flattered at being offered such an intimacy by a man much older than I was. He might be a bit mad, but he obviously had great life experience. Perhaps it was also the setting. The night sky was full of stars. The Doctor was leaning back in his chair, almost a silhouette, like some disembodied spirit recalling storybook memories. After all, I thought, this had been an unusual conversation. I had never had one like it. I suddenly realized that it would never come again and I mustn't miss it. So I almost begged him. 'Yes. Tell me. Please!'

'I said I'd been in China, didn't I?' I nodded and he went on. 'Back in the twenties, to a young man it seemed incredibly romantic. Everything was the opposite of the West. Mourners wore white, the writing went up and down. Policemen tried to scare away thieves not catch them. It was like those pictures on their screens. A fairytale world of byegone days, The Forbidden City, The Temple of Heaven, The Marble Boat! The camel trains, the rickshaws, the teeming life in it all!' He paused again, full of memory. 'More by luck than anything else I happened to be drawn into the company of western sinalogues and through them, I met the young Emperor. Nice boy. I met him twice and it was at the second of these Audiences, when I happened to mention I was going to the Western Hills, that he became very interested and told me I must go to a famous Temple where he had a friend, a relative of his, a certain Prince Hui, who lived there, spoke a few words of English and would, he was certain, be pleased to see me. There and then he called for brush and paper and wrote, in that beautiful calligraphy, a letter of introduction, sealed it with the Imperial Seal, and gave it to me.

'I was naturally delighted. The whole thing began to take on the air of a pilgrimage. During the eighteenth century hundreds of Temples had been built in the Western Hills.

Most of them were now in ruins, abandoned, but even so they had a remarkable atmosphere. In those days there were no roads and you had to travel on foot or hire a donkey train. We had fourteen of them – with bells on their hooves! Imagine! – to get to the Temple, Che Tai Ssu, which lay buried in the folds of the mountains.

'It was the deep tranquillity of these places that first attracted me to Buddhism, which I studied for many years. It is a very quiet religion, with its emphasis on inner peace and meditation ... However that is by the way. I only mention it here because I think that unless I and the friend who was with me wished to enter the Eightfold Path, we should never have been allowed to see ... what we did see.

'Anyway we arrived at the temple one autumn evening with our boys and all our baggage and settled into the little courtyard set aside for guests. Magical place. So silent, so hidden, so far from any world we knew, we hardly dared speak above a whisper. The young Emperor had certainly sent us somewhere very special ...'

The old Doctor paused again and turned to me with an affectionate expression. 'Ah, Jude! What a privilege to be able to talk to a sympathetic listener about the wonders of one's youth! Of what use is old age? Why does one go on? Everything worthwhile is over.' He laid a hand on my arm. 'Well, there it is ...

'We spent all the next morning exploring. The place was set on different levels and our courtyard was at one end of a long broad terrace. Along it were many temples. They were all laid out the same, four low buildings under their curling roofs, one on each side of a courtyard, divided by high walls, with an entrance in the middle of the south wall. There were temples for novices, temples for the laity, temples for storing drums or dragons, courtyards for the priests, for the Abbot, and even one little octagonal shrine reserved for the Emperor Ch'ien Lung himself when he came to meditate here. The whole terrace was shaded with the huge white pines of north

China and their scent in the warm sun was exhilarating, as if the very air was special, as if one was breathing spiritual health!

'I am sure our introduction from the young Emperor had a lot to do with the way we were received. Prince Hui greeted us most courteously and introduced us to the Abbot, a splendid old man over six feet tall. It was he who showed us the temple treasures and took us to see the stupas, those curiously carved stone pagodas about twenty feet tall where the Abbots are all buried upright! Did you know? One was evidently recently completed. The last Abbot had only just died and been buried here. He was a very holy man.

'It was next morning, quite early, when much to our surprise, the young Prince presented himself. He apologized elaborately for disturbing us at such an hour, but went on to explain that a special ceremony was to be held that evening for the Abbot who had recently died. Certain friends of his, closest to him in life, would bring him back.

'Bring him back! I remember how the phrase sharpened our attention to needle point. He spoke quite laconically and went on to say that he knew we were serious people, on the way to following their beliefs and had therefore asked the Abbot for permission for us to be present at the ceremony – if we wished. There was only one proviso – we must not touch food until it was over – but of course we could drink tea. As much tea as we wished, he smiled!

'Have you ever fasted?'

I said that I had not. 'Nor had I until that day. Strange how much we count on meals! "Before lunch", "after tea", "until dinner"! They punctuate our day. Cut them out and it seems endless, a monotony of emptiness. You have no more thoughts to think, as it were. Joe, my Boy, kept on bringing us pots of tea; but by the evening we couldn't look at it! Of course we speculated endlessly about the ceremony. What it would be like, what we should see, what it could possibly mean "to bring him back".

47

'It was night before the Prince came for us. I must say the day had been very long and we were glad to see him. He took us to the main temple where the ceremony was to be held. A huge Buddha towered up into the painted rafters. He was, I think, made of plaster, painted and highly varnished to a rich chestnut colour, which took the candlelight like gold. He was seated on his lotus throne. Hundreds of petals curled up under him, rather like an artichoke, and on the tip of each leaf stood a tiny replica of himself. He smiled that all-knowing smile over the altar where two big red candles stood on tall brass stands and there were the usual receptacles for joss sticks and so on.

'The rest of the temple was perfectly empty. Just a stone flagged floor and the dull oxblood colour of the fretted wall panels covered with rice paper. Lit only by the two candles, the whole place was dim and mysterious. A strong scent of incense filled the air and we sat cross-legged on the floor at the back against the wall as the Prince had instructed us and as for our "wandering thoughts" he smiled, we should try to think as little as we could and pray for the ceremony to reach its fulfilment.

'As our eyes became accustomed to the gloom, we made out four priests, robed in yellow, seated on the floor before the altar. They were facing each other, two either side. They sat, absolutely motionless and erect before the brooding presence of the Buddha and each held something in his hand.

'Behind them, facing the altar, sat a row of younger priests, dressed in grey. I suppose they were novices who had been permitted to be present. The Prince took his place with them. At the back we looked over the whole strange scene. Soon the whole place settled onto what I can only describe as solid silence. Nothing moved. The faces, as far as we could see them were composed, eyes closed. But there was nothing sleepy about the atmosphere. It was alive, pregnant with attention that grew and grew into a sort of expectant power. Somewhere a drum started beating, slow

48

and steady, softly, like a heart. Then a voice began to chant somewhere in the darkness. It went on monotonously, endlessly – and we just sat and waited.

'I'm not used to sitting cross-legged. My legs began to ache, intolerably. Then they went quite numb and I didn't feel them anymore. How long did we sit there? I have often thought about it. Two hours, three, four . . .? I have no idea. Time seemed to have stopped. I longed for it to be over. I didn't care what happened. Then, miraculously, all the pain and discomfort cleared and I felt I could sit there forever. And still nothing . . .'

Suddenly, maddeningly, I heard Father Gregory's voice behind us. 'Ah, there you are!' He pulled up a chair and sat. 'I took Mrs Caesar into Jerusalem to see the Shrine of the Book. Fascinating! Took hours to get back. No lights, for some reason.'

I just stared at him, furious at the interruption.

'Must be night manoeuvres on,' he went on. 'Strings of trucks, tank transporters, guns . . . Looked like general mobilization. I wonder what's up.'

CHAPTER FIVE

10.10.73. It's difficult to get back into the mood of that evening, here, in London. But I still remember my irritation. All the atmosphere that the Doctor had created had been swamped by Father Gregory's intrusion. Of course it wasn't his fault. He didn't know what we'd been talking about. In fact I suppose if we had paid more attention to his remarks, we might have made inquiries. But we didn't. Instead we just chatted about the efficiency of the Israeli army. A moment or two later I excused myself, said goodnight to the Doctor, thanked him for a wonderful evening and went up to my room.

I found I couldn't sleep. I lay awake for a long time, envying him for those days, for having had the luck to live in a mediaeval society, in a way of life that had now completely disappeared. I began to reflect how modern life had burst over the world in the last fifty years. In a flash! Now all the magic had gone . . . I dozed off . . .

I don't know how long I'd been asleep when the phone rang. I woke with a start, without realizing what it was – and was irritated when I did. Who on earth could be ringing me at this hour?

'Hullo! Is that you, Heddon?' It was Father Gregory's voice. I told him, curtly, that it was. 'I do apologize for disturbing you, but something extraordinary has happened. Really extraordinary . . . and I thought you might be able to help – if you would.'

'What is it?'

'Well, you won't believe me, but an Arab, only a kid

really, actually barged into Mrs Caesar's room half an hour ago – luckily I was there, talking with her. (And what were you doing there at two o'clock in the morning? I thought.) She was scared, always on edge about being hijacked – but the kid only grinned and made friendly gestures and showed us a bundle of rags. When he began to unroll them, I saw – I could hardly believe my eyes – a roll of blackened leather. It was a scroll, a Dead Sea Scroll. Imagine! Absolutely unheard of! Fabulous!'

'Extraordinary!'

'The kid jabbered away about his mother, very sick, trouble in the family, no money, the usual story, but I noticed Mrs Caesar was as excited as I was – we'd just come back from looking at the Scrolls in the Shrine – so I cut him short and held out my hand for the scroll; but he wouldn't let go of it, just opened it enough for me to see the script. How much? I said. He made signs with his fingers, two, five and said "tousand". He was very jumpy all the time, kept looking round at the door. Maybe he's stolen the thing. But of course that sort of money for a scroll is peanuts, ridiculous . . .'

'If it's genuine.'

'No doubt about that. Impossible to fake these things. Anyhow Mrs Caesar wrote out a cheque for $25,000 and gave it to him. I don't think he'd ever seen a cheque before. Money, money, he kept saying, want money. I told him Money. Bank. Tomorrow morning. So, finally, he pushed the scroll into my hands, grabbed the cheque and bolted.'

I was wide awake now. 'How on earth did anyone know Mrs Caesar was here?'

'Don't ask me. Some sort of grapevine. The woman's internationally known, of course. Maybe the night porter is a relative, or one of the waiters . . . Anyhow the point is that as, by pure luck, you happen to be here, could you possibly come over and photograph it? Then at least we'd have a copy . . .'

'Photograph the writing you mean?'

'Yes. You see this sort of thing has happened before.
Scrolls, or bits of them, turn up and then there is some sort
of family vendetta or something and they just disappear
again. You see the boy coming late at night, well, it's a bit
fishy. Anything can happen.'

'Maybe the boy's just pulling a fast one.'

'Maybe. It's possible. It's in wonderful condition, Heddon.
The end's all blackened with damp, of course, but one must
expect that, after two thousand years, but inside! It might
have been written yesterday. So, if you possibly can, don't
refuse. These things are so rare, so important, so sacred
really, we have a sort of obligation, if you see what I mean,
not to take any chances. Can you manage it?'

'Well, I'd like to have a look at it first.'

'Of course.' He gave me his room number.

'I'll be over as soon as I can.'

I'd already been thinking while he talked. Close-up lens,
black and white, electronic flash. I had the gear. So I pulled
on a dressing gown, loaded a camera, tested the flash, picked
up a tripod and went along.

In the room I found Greg and the Doctor. Both were in
dressing gowns. Greg's was grey and ordinary, but the
Doctor's was a highly coloured, flamboyant affair. It made
him look like a Rajah and introduced a cheerful, almost comic
note into the scene. Greg was evidently in a great state,
jumpy and nervous, and together, at either end of the little
glass-topped writing table, they were attempting to open the
scroll between them. Greg was all the time admonishing the
Doc to be careful, for heaven's sake, not to pull on it, not to
strain it, not to break it, and so on, while the Doc, good-
humouredly, kept his mouth shut and his concentration on
his fingers. They greeted me almost absentmindedly, deeply
absorbed in what they were doing and it gave me a chance to
look at what I'd come to photograph. I'd never seen a scroll
before. It was a roll of yellowish looking paper, parchment I
suppose, about ten inches or a foot across and several feet

52

long. The end – it turned out to be the outer end – was under the Doc's fingers. It had evidently become stained in the course of time and was very dark brown, almost black in colour. The stain had seeped through on one side to the inner part of the scroll, so that what was written on it was blotted out every so often where the damp had penetrated. Perhaps this damp had kept the whole thing a bit soft and enabled them to unroll it. Anyway they seemed to be managing it and when I got there the Doc had placed a Bible – evidently Father Gregory's bedside reading – over his end, holding it flat, and was sliding the whole thing towards him, slowly and carefully, while Greg let the inner end unroll under his fingers where it was coiled like a watchspring. The bit that lay flat on the table was covered in columns of characters, black and clear, but in a strange sort of writing I had never seen before.

'Is it Hebrew?' I asked.

'No. Aramaic,' Greg replied, 'and I don't read it, more's the pity. So I've no idea what's on it. Now, Heddon, could you get that bit?'

Between them they had opened up about two feet of the scroll on the table top. At either end and in the middle were the broad dark stained patches, but between the script was clear. I told them it was impossible. I couldn't handhold the camera that close. It had to be steady, accurately focused. An inch one way or the other would make all the difference.

They had evidently never thought I wouldn't be able to do it. For the first time they stopped and looked at me.

'Then what are we to do? I'm terrified it will crack or break or just disintegrate. They often do. We'll be left with nothing but dust . . .'

It was a problem. I could see no way of fixing the camera vertically over the top of the thing.

'Could you unroll it against the wall?'

'No, no. Daren't risk it. It would be inexcusable to break

the thing up. The chaps in the scrollery would never forgive me.'

There was a pause. We would have to improvise something.

'Have you got a suitcase?' I asked.

'Yes.'

'Then if you could open it on the top of that, flat, we might be able to tilt the whole thing against the wall. That would probably do.'

Father Gregory was doubtful and anxious, but, after we had talked it over and got out the suitcase and rehearsed the way the two of them would lift it, he agreed. 'It's the only possible way,' I told him.

So then, very gently, they let the two ends of the scroll roll up together, slid a newspaper under it and gingerly laid it down on the bed. I saw Father Gregory was sweating with suppressed anxiety and excitement. 'Terrified to touch it,' he said, almost to himself. 'Two thousand years old, if it's a day. If it's too difficult, we simply mustn't risk it. Now, show me how you mean.'

I took the suitcase from him and laid it against the wall at an angle, the bottom edge on the table top.

'It'll slip on the glass,' said the Doctor, 'better get a towel.'

Father Gregory spread a towel on the table top. We laid the suitcase against the wall. The Doc looked at it, then picked up a pair of Greg's shoes and wedged them under the bottom. He tried it. 'It won't shift now,' he said.

'We'd better try it,' said Father Gregory.

I told them it would be better if I got set up first, so I pulled out the tripod legs, screwed on the camera and got a focus on the Doc's hand on the suitcase top. I had to come in pretty close. But it would work, I thought, if they could manage the scroll. I tested the flash and we were ready to go.

Thinking it over, here, a few days later, back in my flat, it made me smile. If anybody had come in, it would really have looked a strange scene! The bare hotel room, the flat top light, the clothes lying about, the disordered bed and the three of us in our dressing gowns, clustered round a dirty old bit of paper, photographing it on a suitcase top! At one side the Doctor, his fingers curling over his end as if it was an egg; at the other Greg slowly pulling open his end and me between them squinting through the viewfinder. 'There!' Father Gregory would say. 'There! Is that enough? Get that bit.' And I would ask for an inch more, or move the camera, refocus and show with my hand how much we were covering. 'Okay, Uncle Jon, pull off your end now, gently, for our dear Lord's sake. Let it roll up. That's it.'

In half an hour we had come to the inner end of the scroll. I had taken a dozen shots or so, covering the whole thing, except the beginning, the blackened bit, which was almost half its length. That, I told them, might show something with infra red. 'Okay,' I said. 'That's it. Let me get out of your way.'

I lifted the camera clear and laid it on the bed.

'Could you get those shoes out and help us to get the case flat?' Father Gregory asked, 'It'll be easier to roll up that way.'

Together we managed it. When, finally, it was safely rolled up again, Father Gregory sat down, exhausted. 'Phew! Never thought it would stand it. Thank the Lord we've got it and not damaged a thing. I can't thank you enough, Heddon. Wonderful job. Now, whatever happens, there's a record.'

'I wonder what's on it, after all that,' I said.

'I've no idea. We'll have to wait until Allegro or Yadim or one of the experts gives us a translation. But it's in such wonderful condition – except for the damp patches, as good as Isaiah.' He carefully wrapped it back in its dirty cloths. 'Fantastic that boy turning up like that. Wonder if we'll be able to get it out of the country. There might be difficulties . . .'

I had been packing up my gear and was just about to say goodnight and leave when the phone rang.

'Now what is it?' Father Gregory lifted the receiver and we could hear Julia Caesar's voice shouting at the other end. 'Father Gregory? For God's sake come over right away, will you? There's another guy here, says I've stolen that scroll. Says it doesn't belong to the boy. Bring it back right away! I'm scared.'

'At once.' Father Gregory hung up. He looked at us. 'You heard? What did I say?' He picked up the scroll. 'She sounds in quite a state. Well, we got it anyway.' He crossed to the door. 'I won't be long.'

I said I would take the gear back to my room and then come back to join the Doctor and hear what had happened. He had stretched out on the bed. 'Greg's such a *busy* man,' he sighed. 'Tires me out. Always doing something, fixing something, planning something, or stopping something . . . It must be my age. It exhausts me!'

'Well, take it easy until I get back,' I told him.

'Until he gets back, you mean!' He laughed as I went out of the door.

I was just coming back along the corridor when I was surprised to see the Manager. 'Good evening, sir,' he said politely but hurriedly. 'Are you leaving at once? We'll do what we can to get you a taxi, but it won't be easy.'

I was completely mystified. 'Leaving?' I said. 'Probably some time tomorrow perhaps, but . . .'

He cut in. 'Then you haven't heard the news? Egypt has attacked across the Canal. The Syrians have overrun the Golan Heights. We are at war!'

11.10.73. Annie wants a rise. Prices are terrible, she says. Had to give it to her; but it set me thinking and I went round to the bank to see how I stood. As usual I found I'd spent more than I intended. I'd counted on getting this new book away pretty quickly and the advance would tide me over until my next trip. It isn't the way I like to live, but what can one do? I shall have to be careful. No taxis!

Read through the last entry. Suppose I must tidy it all up by finishing off the details of the trip. Not much to add really. When I got back to Father Gregory's room and told the Doctor the news, he was up off the bed in a jiffy.

'Fascinating!' he said. 'Fascinating!'

It wasn't the reaction I'd expected. 'We'll have to get out,' I said.

'Of course. Of course. They won't have much use for tourists hanging around.' He paused, smiling more to himself than me. 'But isn't it fascinating? Ever since '67 Egypt's been talking about war – and always putting it off, until we reached the point that nobody believed it, or took it seriously, anyway. Could it have been a deeply laid plan? To cry Wolf! Is Sadat that clever? And on the holiest day of the year! I wonder if they've caught Israel on the hop? Now we know what those convoys Greg saw were up to!'

A moment later Greg came back into the room, rather hurriedly, and closed the door. 'Heard the news?' the Doctor asked him. Greg nodded. I don't think he'd really taken it in.

'That man was a ruffian, a thug. I think if I hadn't turned up, he'd have attacked poor Mrs Caesar. He was convinced she'd stolen the thing. When he saw it in my hand, he snatched it away from me, like an animal. I tried to explain; but he didn't really listen. The boy who'd been round earlier was with him, obviously frightened, cowering behind him. He was an ugly customer. I said we might be interested in purchasing the scroll. That met with a torrent of Arabic, most of which was too quick for me; but I think he was saying it was already sold, sold to America. He turned on the boy. The boy had stolen it. It belonged to him, to his family. He seemed very excited. I asked him how much he had been offered. We might be able to meet the price, I said. But he wouldn't listen.

' "Now war. War," he kept saying. "Soon finish. Then more money. More. Much more." I saw we were getting nowhere so I told him the boy must return the cheque Mrs

Caesar had given him. He turned on the lad again, who answered violently. He had nothing. No money, no cheque. Nothing. Obviously the man believed him, or pretended to, anyway. "Thieves," he said, "you are thieves. You steal. You tell lies." Then I'm afraid I got very angry. I told him to get out, sharp. For a moment I thought he would come at me; but he evidently thought better of it, just turned, flung open the door, kicked the boy through it muttering, "Thieves! Liars! Christian scum!", banged it behind him and that was that. Very pretty! But he'll come round, of course – if we offer him enough . . .'

'And if you can find him,' the Doctor put in.

'Oh, we'll find him. These people all know each other. If there's money, he'll turn up.'

I must say I wondered, but the Doctor cut in about the war. What, he inquired, did Greg think of the news? Father Gregory was sure it was exaggerated. Just a scare. Egypt had been belly-aching about fighting for years. But they had no guts. They wouldn't risk it. They'd find themselves worse off than before. Anyway there was nothing to be done until morning. On that note we went to bed.

But next morning the situation was all too plain. The hotel was pretty well deserted. All the staff – the men and most of the women – had gone. We managed to get a cup of coffee and make ourselves some toast in the kitchens. There were two old girls there. Cleaners I think. Greg offered me a lift into Jerusalem. He did the same for Mrs Caesar – she greeted me warmly as if that awful scene had never happened. Extraordinary woman! Very slow trip. All the roads choked with cars, trucks, men singing as they went to their posts. I must say the morale seemed terrific. 'Damascus next week!' they shouted. When at last we got there, we split up. Father Gregory was going to stay on for a day or two to see how it went. The Doctor aimed to return to the UK via Rome where he had to see somebody. Mrs Caesar was rejoining her friends. (She gave me her card with her New

York address, telling me to be sure to look her up if I came to the States! What a hope!) Father Gregory gave me his address and I promised to forward the photos to him in Rome as soon as I'd developed them. After waiting about a bit, I managed to get a ride down to Tel-Aviv and finally humped my suitcase and cameras out to the airport. Not funny in the heat! Of course it was closed! So there was nothing to do but wait about. Finally I managed to get a seat . . . The whole thing's been a waste of time and money.

CHAPTER SIX

12.10.73. Sent off my colour rolls for development and did the black and white myself. The scroll shots have come out quite well. Printed them on the enlarger in the afternoon. Plenty of overlap. It would be possible to make a complete mosaic; but there's no point really. So I just numbered them and posted them off to Rome with a brief note to Father Gregory, saying I'd be interested to hear what was on them, when he had time.

15.10.73. Doctor Ramsay phoned. Just back in town. He asked me to lunch and I went along, wondering whether I'd like him in a 'home' setting. People you meet on trips often turn out to be dreadful when you're back! He gave me a very good lunch (Simpsons) and I found him just as entertaining as ever. Lively mind and a stimulating way with him. I found him still enthusiastic about the Israelis. 'Another week and they'll be in Cairo – if America lets them!' We swapped yarns about how we got out of Tel-Aviv.

I took him back to the flat to see the prints of the famous scroll. He told me Greg had already taken them to the 'experts' before he left Rome and hoped to get some idea of what was on them soon. I showed him the prints and he was amazed how good they were, considering how we got them! We laughed together over that bedroom scene. 'Real Secret Service stuff!' he said. 'Nobody would believe it ever happened!'

I settled him in the chair in my big bay window, privately planning to ask him questions. That scene in the Chinese Temple had remained vividly in my mind, but I feared he might regret having spoken of it, regret having been indiscreet perhaps about something very esoteric, very private, which ought not to be known. So I started by telling him, in quite a casual way, how I'd always been fascinated by China – old China – and how lucky I thought him to have been able to live in all that, before it disappeared forever.

'Yes. You can't imagine how rich it was! Everything! Even the life of the streets, Lantern Street, Jade Street, Kingfisher Feather Street, the endless maze of the so-called Chinese City, outside the Walls. And the Walls themselves! You could march twelve abreast on them! All round! With the Gatehouses at the corners, deserted, thick with dust and thousands of bats! And the theatres! Huge! All made of scaffolding and straw mats. Terrific fire hazard! And the plays going on for days at a time, nobody paying much attention. Families camping in the stalls, chatting, spitting sunflower seeds, sipping tea, calling for hot towels which kids lobbed to them right across the auditorium! It was wonderful! Such a gush of life! Endless, endless . . . All gone now, quite, quite gone . . .'

He'd been staring out of the window and now sighed deeply. 'You know, Jude, the worst of it is we took it all for granted. We thought it would be the same forever! And in a couple of decades it was gone! But in those days there was no hurry. There was ease. Time. Leisure. You could browse. You didn't have to rush about 'doing things'. Now we must have everything at once. Instant coffee, instant wealth, instant love! We know the price of everything and the value of nothing, as Wilde said.'

'It sounds marvellous,' I said, and then, changing key, 'and were there many temples where you could run into a ceremony like the one you described – you know I was furious when Greg butted in that evening at En Gedi. I've been longing to hear how it ended.'

'Yes.' He was reflective. 'I never finished, did I? Well . . .' He paused, staring into space, as if trying to recreate in his mind the state he had felt on that faraway night in the

61

Temple . . . 'I told you the silence had enveloped us for hours, as it seemed, and nothing happened. I think we were tired, dazed and a bit hypnotized perhaps when it did happen. The monotonous chanting, the throbbing drum, the sense of expectancy of a moment that never seemed to arrive. I felt I must have blinked, or dozed, or gone blank for a second and so had somehow missed the very moment when he did arrive. For that was all it was. The old Abbot was suddenly just standing there before the altar between the four monks. The moment before there had been nothing, now there was, emanating an extraordinary atmosphere of serenity and peace. It took a second or two for me to take it in, to realize I was seeing what I saw – a miracle – and to feel a mixture of elation and awe at the old man's dignity and authority. His right hand was raised as if giving a blessing, his left held a book. A scarlet cloak hung from one shoulder over his orange robes. In the dim candlelight, the whole thing looked sculptured, almost unreal, except his face which bore an expression of absolute peace and content. It was quite beautiful. I felt an emotion of joy floating through everybody, a whisper of wonder!

'Then he spoke, quietly for a moment, as if inviting the priests to speak. They did, asking something which the old man answered, each one in turn. Then that immense silence came back and after a moment, the old man raised his hand again. He seemed to be praying over all of us. Then he turned, bowed low before the great Buddha and, as he did so, disappeared.

'For quite a long time nobody moved. Then the young priests got up and quietly filed out. The four in the yellow robes followed. At last we managed to stumble to our feet. My legs were quite numb from the ordeal and we staggered to the doorway, stepped over the high threshold onto the terrace, where the young Prince was waiting for us. "Eat a little now," he said, "Not too much." Well, as you can imagine, we weren't up very early next morning!'

He finished lightly enough, but the impression was profound. I was excited by it all and full of questions I felt I wanted to ask and yet knew couldn't be answered.

'Did you have a chance to ask the Prince about it afterwards?'

'Yes, of course we were full of questions. But we didn't get anywhere much with them. Why had they held the ceremony? Because there were important questions about the Teaching they wanted answered. Did they get them? Of course. Could they repeat the ritual and ask other questions? If it was necessary. How was it done? You saw how it was done, they smiled. And there you are! You can't get any further because to know the powers they exercised you would have to have those powers yourself. It wasn't just a stunt. They knew what to do, but it was their need that made them do it.'

'I asked him if he believed in the so-called "black box". If you give a medium something belonging to the person, a letter, a lock of hair – even if they're the other side of the world – they can tell you how that person is, their health, their circumstances, whether they're alive or dead. There's a sort of thread joining a man to the parts of himself he's discarded, they say. It sounds crazy, I said, but somehow I've often wondered whether there isn't something in it.

"Oh, I think there is," he answered at once. "This is the reason people used to collect relics. Now they're just curiosities; but it used to spring from the same idea. If you have a bone or a tooth or a hair of a saint, you can make contact with the saint – if you know how!"

"That's the snag!"

'It all comes back to belief. To need – and love. Those priests were each carrying something, probably something belonging to their teacher. That was the end of the thread. But how you pull on the thread? Ah, there's the mystery. All you can say is that certain people do seem to acquire special powers, outside normal experience. If you've seen them at work you know they're possible. But how they've acquired remain the secrets of those who have them ... We have to leave it at that.'

17.10.73. The Doc phoned. Quite excited. He'd had Greg on the phone. 'The photos were unique, he said, or rather the original Scroll was "Sensational!" That was the word he used. And when Greg gets to the point of using words like that there must be something in it. He's writing to you.'

He suggested we went along to the Chinese Exhibition, so I met him there and we fought our way round in the crowd. The worst thing – and the thing most publicized – was that awful jade suit of funeral mail. What vulgarity! Compared with the Egyptian things this was a definite non-starter.

Went back to have a cup of tea with the Doctor – in the Abbey, of all places! Got a friend who works there, as he put it. Nice, cosy flat in the Precincts. Quiet. In the very heart of London. View of Big Ben over the roof tops. Big chairs. Walls lined with books. 'Something to be said for the Church,' he smiled. 'The perks are very pleasant – when you get to the top.'

I asked if he lived here permanently. 'Oh, no. Only when I'm over. I've spent the last seven years of my life in India, but I've finished my stint there now, tired of lecturing young hopefuls on the merits of comparative religions.'

I was interested. I told him what I most wanted to compare was the relation of art to religion. All the greatest art, it seemed to me, sprung from religion, but it didn't tell you much about it. It only suggested there might be something there. A red herring, so to speak.

'Mm. I don't see it quite like that. To me Art is a sort of offering. The artist believes in something. He doesn't know quite what it is, but he creates a glimpse of what he thinks it is. The great temples, the glorious sculptures are offerings to God, his way to make the invisible visible. Compulsive.'

'Do you believe in reincarnation?' I don't know why I

64

fired the question at him so unexpectedly. I suppose I felt that he'd studied these things more than I had and maybe he had the answer. I've always had the question knocking about in the back of my mind. He didn't answer at once and I went on: 'There's nothing about it in the Gospels.'

'I think it's only a question of emphasis. The Christian emphasis is all on this life. Live in a certain way and you will be rewarded with life in the hereafter. Those who believe in reincarnation say: You have lived before and you will live again and your next life depends on the way you live this one. So, what's the difference? The danger is not to take care of this life because you've got another one coming! Do these things bother you?'

'In a way. I suppose I had religion stuffed down my throat so much when I was a kid, I've always got a sort of guilt complex: not having bothered, not behaving as I ought to behave and, oh, I don't know . . .'

'My dear Jude, it's no good worrying about that! We all do what we can, live as our conscience dictates, hope for the best and leave it at that! Have another cup of tea!'

When I left him to go home, I found I was still depressed, all the same. Why do I get these moods? I suppose it's being thwarted about the Israeli trip. The whole thing was a waste of time and money. And I can't afford it.

CHAPTER SEVEN

18.10.73. Found a letter from Father Gregory in the post. After reading it, decided to include the whole thing in my diary.

My dear Jude Heddon,

I am sure you will be interested to hear that the splendid photographs you took of the scroll that was offered to Mrs Caesar are of the greatest possible importance. My colleagues here have made a first rough translation (attached) from which you will see that the original scroll appears to be a Fifth Gospel! It is an extraordinary and unbelievable piece of luck! More than the first half was ruined, as you know, but what we have is an account, in itself incomplete, of the last days of our Lord's life and Resurrection. You can imagine what this new light on the Passion will mean to the whole of Christendom. It is tragic that so little has remained undisfigured, but we hope, if we can find and purchase the original, much may be done by modern methods to decipher those passages in the narrative which have been ruined by damp. Meanwhile we must be grateful for small mercies. Even what your photos reveal is enough not only to give additional proof of Jesus' earthly life as a historical figure – and thus silence the cynics and doubters – like dear Uncle Jon – but also to shed new light on the mysteries of the Resurrection.

I am leaving for Israel today to do all I possibly can to run the scroll to earth and obtain possession of it. Meanwhile, may I ask you to guard the negatives most carefully, since they may be — if I fail to locate the scroll — the only record of this sensational document? It is most important at this stage that nothing should appear in the press or any rumour of this great discovery should be known. It would raise the price to an impossible level.

FIRST ROUGH TRANSLATION

made into English, of fragments of a Scroll, written in Aramaic, purporting to come from the Dead Sea area, photos of which were shown to us by Father Gregory on his return from a recent visit to Israel.

N.B. Although the photographic record is clear, much of the text is obliterated by damp which has penetrated deep into the scroll and blots it out at irregular intervals. Where words in the text are mutilated or unclear a provisional meaning is given. Where the text approximates to that of other Gospels, these have been used.

A revised translation will follow later.

'. . . and they spread their garments on the road before Him.

Now when He came to the Mount of Olives a great multitude met Him, praising God for the miracles they had seen and crying "Blessings on the King who comes in the Lord's name! Peace in Heaven! Hosanna in the highest!"

And when He arrived in Jerusalem, the whole city was astonished. "Who is this man?" they said.

And the people answered. "This is Jesus, the prophet from Nazareth in Galilee."

And they that were with Him told how He had called Lazarus from his grave and raised him from the dead.

Then the crowds ran towards Him to see the man that had done this.

And Jesus taught them, saying: "I am the way, the truth and the life. He who . . ."'

Passage obliterated

'Then Jesus entered the Temple and raged against them

that bought and sold there and threw down the tables of the money changers and them that sold doves.

And He upbraided them: "It is written my house shall be called a house of prayer; but ye have made it a thieves' market."

Then the priests when they heard this grew fearful for they saw that the people worshipped Him.

So the Elders and the Pharisees called a council. "If we stand aside," they said, "the whole city will follow Him and when we who uphold the Law rebuke them, there will be riots. It will come to bloodshed. Jewry will be brought into derision and the Romans will crush our faith."

Then one of them named Caiaphas, who was High Priest that year, cried out: "We have talked enough. This man must be crucified. It is expedient that one man die for the people."

So they made plans to arrest Him.

But this they dared not do openly, for the city was on fire for Him. So they sent out spies pretending to be His followers, to twist His words and then to accuse Him of blasphemy and bring Him before the Governor.

And these men set about to trap Him saying: "Master we know you speak truth without respect for persons and teach the way of God. Is it lawful for us to give tribute to Caesar or not?"

But Jesus saw their guile and said: "Why do you set snares for me? Shew me a penny. Whose head and titles are stamped upon it?"

They answered: "Caesar's."

Then Jesus answered them, saying: "Give to Caesar what is due to Caesar and to God what is due to Him."

His answer dumbfounded them and they were silent.'

Passage obliterated

'Now Simon, the father of Judas Iscariot worked in the Temple and Caiaphas called him and said: "Is not thy son

68

one of those that follow this Jesus?" Simon answered him: "I know not." Then Caiaphas said: "Bring your son before me that I may question him."

And when Judas stood before him, the Chief Priest said: "Are you one of those that follow this fellow called Jesus?"

And Judas answered: "I am."

Then the Chief priest and the Elders began to revile him, calling him traitor and blasphemer and threatened to put him to the torture if he did not betray Him, promising him thirty pieces of silver if he would lead the guard to the place where He could be taken secretly.

Then Judas, seeing a way into their councils, said: "I will do it."

And when Judas came to the Twelve and told them of it, they were dismayed and begged Jesus not to go about the city but to withdraw into the country. So they went to a place called Ephraim and remained there together.

Now the Disciples became suddenly afraid and said to each other: "If some dreadful thing were to befall the Lord and He were to be taken from us, could we keep His commandments, could we teach His truths?"

But Jesus, knowing their thoughts, said: "Be not afraid for the end is not yet." And He called them close about Him and taught them, saying: "Take no thought for the morrow. Sufficient it is to be here. Now, be still and know that I am God. Tomorrow will take care of itself."'

Passage obliterated

'. . . and when the guards had looked diligently for the Lord and found Him not, they conferred among themselves and doubled their numbers against the day when He would return to Jerusalem.

Now two days before the Feast of the Passover Jesus came back to the city with His disciples and spent all day in the Temple.

Great crowds pressed about Him. And they brought Him

their lepers, their sick, their blind and those not in their right minds. And He healed them.

Nor did He in those days refuse any man anything.

But the Chief Priest, seeing all this was beside himself and said: "The whole world is gone mad about this impostor. There must be an end of it. He is inspired by devils and by Beelzebub casts them out. Can any good thing come out of Galilee? Who will destroy this fanatic for me?"

But those about him said: "We have no power to put any man to death. If you do this you will answer to the Governor for it."

Then Caiaphas answered. "It is the custom at the Passover for the Governor to grant us a petition. Let us beg him to release the murderer Barabbas and crucify this criminal in his place." And having agreed it among themselves, the Chief Priest exhorted the guards and promised gifts of gold to any who should take Him.

Now Jesus, to whom all things were known, said to Judas and John: "Go into the city and prepare the Passover that we may eat together."

But Judas besought Him, saying: "Master, the windows have eyes and ears. The guards go from house to house."

Then Jesus said: "Nevertheless go. And when you meet a man bearing a pail of water, follow him. And when he enters his house say to him: 'The Master asks have you a room where we may hold the Passover with friends?' And he will show you an upper room. There make ready. And admonish the master of the house that he say nothing of this, and you, as you come and go, seek not to be seen of men."

So Judas and John did as He had directed them and made ready the Passover and Jesus came and sat and the Twelve with Him.

And Jesus said: "I have desired to eat this Passover with you before I suffer. For the hour approaches when the Son of Man shall be delivered to the Gentiles to be mocked *and scourged and crucified. But on the third day he will return to you alive from the dead."*

Then seeing them distraught with grief, Jesus had pity on them and said: "Be not afraid. In my end is my beginning. He who believes in me, even if he be dead, shall live."

Then having prayed, He took a knife and cut flesh from His body and divided it among them, a portion to each, and allowed His blood to drip into a cup and passed it to each of them saying: "He that eats of my flesh and drinks of my blood may call on me and on my Father which sent me, and I will come to him even from the dead and lead him on the path to life everlasting."

And as He began to share the cup among them, there came a heavy knocking at the lower door.

Then Judas, knowing it to be the guard and what had to be done, sprang up. And Jesus blessed him and bid him go.

And Judas ran down to greet the guards saying: "I have just had word where your man is hiding. Come, follow me quickly. There is no time to waste."

And he led them about the city from house to house, but they found . . .'

Passage obliterated

'. . . knowing that he was deceived, bound Judas and took him before the Chief Priest and said: "This man makes light of us. He is a traitor. All night he has taken us from house to house and we have found nothing."

Then said Caiaphas: "Scourge him."

And when it was done, Judas confessed: "At midnight He will be at Gethsemane. If He be not, let my life be forfeit."

Then said the haughty Caiaphas: "Take him, bound, and if this Jesus be not found, bring him back to me. I shall know how to reward him."

And when they came to Gethsemane Judas said: "Loose me now and follow me. The man I kiss will be He."

And as soon as He saw him Jesus sprang up and came to Judas and embraced him, saying: "My son! My son! For this thou shalt be sanctified in Paradise!"

And Judas kissed Him and fell at His feet saying: "My Lord and my God!"

Then the Guard with their staves and lanterns crowded around Jesus and said: "Art thou the man called Jesus, the Nazarene?" And He answered: "I am."

And immediately they took Him and bound Him. But the Disciples, as He had commanded them, deserted Him and fled.'

Long passage obliterated

'. . . and they came to the house of which Jesus had spoken and went in and prayed earnestly together, for they were heavy with grief.

And as they prayed, there stood Jesus in the midst of them. And He blessed them saying: "Peace be unto you."

But they were amazed and terrified, thinking it to be a ghost.

Then Jesus said: "Be not afraid. Touch me now and know that it is I myself. For a ghost has not flesh as you see me have."

And they fell at His feet and worshipped Him.

Then Jesus said: "Because you have shared my flesh and blood, you have become part of me and I of you. And I am with you always and forever." Then Peter wept and cried out: "Lord, how can we live without you? Have mercy on our loneliness!"

Jesus said: "Be of good cheer, for I will send you the Holy Spirit, the Comforter, and He shall sustain you. Teach all men what you have learned of me. Freely you have received, freely give. And do not think what to say, for it is not you who speak but my Father that speaks through you. What I have taught you in secret now preach openly, for he that receives you receives me and he that receives me receives Him that sent me.

"Blessed are your eyes that see what you have seen and hear what you have heard, for I say unto you there shall be many prophets and kings that shall long to have seen them and have not and to have heard them and have not."

Then He blessed them and departed.'

Passage obliterated

'And He appeared again to Thomas, the doubter, upbraiding him and saying: "Because you have seen you have believed. Blessed are they who have not seen and yet believe."

And to two other disciples He also appeared walking on the dark road to Emmaus, and taught them, saying: "I am the light of the world. Walk in the light while it is with you, lest the darkness come when no man shall see the road before him."

And to the beloved Mary, the Magdalen, the first to see Him risen, He also appeared and to others . . .'

Passage obliterated

'. . . in the boat were Simon, called Peter, and Thomas and Nathaniel, of Cana, and Judas Iscariot and two other disciples.

And as they came towards the shore they saw a man kindling a fire. Then said Judas to Peter: "It is the Lord!"

And Peter immediately jumped into the sea and took a rope to haul the boat onto the sand.

And when they saw the fire with fish cooking on it, they were overjoyed and fell at His feet and He received them, saying: "Come and dine."

Then He poured wine and took bread and shared it among them and the fish also and said: "I am the bread of life. He that eats with me shall never hunger and he that drinks with me shall never thirst."

And He raised His hands to Heaven and prayed, saying: "Father, I have finished the work you gave me to do. I have taught your Word to the men you gave me out of this world. Yours they are and they been faithful. Sanctify them with your Truth, that they may be one with you as you, Father, are with me and I with you.

Father glorify thy Name!"

And immediately as He said it, came a loud voice out of Heaven saying: "I have glorified it and will glorify it for ever and ever."

Then He stretched out His hands over them and breathed upon them and blessed them, saying: "Feed my sheep. Feed my lambs."

And then He was lifted up and they saw Him no more.'

CHAPTER EIGHT

I sat for a long time after I'd finished reading. I'd never really thought about the Crucifixion before. It had never been real to me. It was just something that happened a long time ago. But now! It had come alive with a vengeance! It grew in my mind. The march of destiny! Something absolutely inescapable, as predetermined as tomorrow's light. Frightening! I couldn't put words to what I felt; but then I came to it – awe. I was awed by it.

For the first time I really saw good and evil at work. The wave of joy that greeted Jesus as He rode into Jerusalem. People carried away by this quiet man who touched them and made them whole. And then the hatred, the jealousy of the priests, seeing something they could not understand, something that might turn dangerous. Fear! There could be riots, fighting in the streets. They must do away with Him. Quickly. Before the Passover. All the tensions rising, whirling round Jesus like a tornado! And He perfectly calm at the centre of it.

What a risk to hold that supper! The joy at being with the Lord against the danger of the house to house searches. Then, sure enough, the knocking on the door, coming at the height of it, and Judas leaping up, the wily little man, always equal to the occasion. He must gain time. Only two hours! Fool the Guard. Follow me! Search these attics! And those cellars! Ten minutes here, half an hour there. Keen, plausible, practical. I need the money! Keep it up until midnight, until Gethsemane. Then, at last, 'Well done, little saint!' and the final fateful kiss. He had been faithful.

After that I couldn't really follow it. It was all to do

with the supernatural, the after life. But that didn't really hold my interest. It was beyond me. I was out of my depth . . .

I'd been feeling pretty low since I got back. These black moods overtake me from time to time. I know I oughtn't to give way to them, but they just drown me. I think it must be metabolic, a sort of illness. Then they pass, thank God, or I should have finished it all, long ago.

Later on, reading over what I'd written, I slowly began to cheer up. I realized what extraordinary luck it was that I should happen to be in on a discovery like this! It grew clearer the more I thought about it. The thing was bound to arouse a lot of interest. Those earlier Scrolls, esoteric as they were, had created quite a stir, but it was mainly technical. But this! A new light on the Crucifixion! Judas as a hero! Yes, it was, as Greg had said, sensational. I began to see the form it might take. A book. My photos. The translation. Perhaps the trip hadn't been wasted. I must show the translation to the Doc. Perhaps I was on to a good thing after all!

I'd just left the negatives hanging in the darkroom. Now they began to be priceless. I took them down, put each one in a separate cellophane envelope, numbered them and locked them away in my old deed box where I keep my contracts, letters from my mother and all my personal things. Nobody knew of their existence except Greg and the Doc; but still . . . better be on the safe side.

Next morning I rang the Doc and told him about Greg's letter and the translation.

'What is it?' he asked. 'A new version of Obadaiah or Habbakuk?' and he laughed.

When I told him it was a sort of fifth gospel, according to Judas, I could feel, even on the phone, it had knocked him for six. He whistled.

'Good God! I can't believe it. According to Judas! It's impossible! Can I see it?'

I told him Greg had suggested I should show it to him — provided he'd keep his mouth shut.

He laughed. 'Trust Greg to make a secret of it! But he's right, of course. To let anything like this get about before we're quite sure it's authentic would be to make absolute fools of ourselves. When can I come round?'

I suggested supper. 'I'll whip you up an omelette,' I said.

'I can hardly wait,' he said. 'D'you realize what this means — if it's authentic. It'll shake the Christian world to its foundations. Fairly set the cat among the pigeons! What a lark!'

I spent the rest of the morning browsing through this diary, thinking how best to present the whole thing. Then I decided to get out another set of prints and match the overlaps to make up a mosaic. It would make a very effective fold-out illustration. The text could be abstracted from it and the 'experts' could then argue about the actual words, make bracketed links, etc. It took me most of the day to mount this up; but it came off and I looked forward to showing it to the Doc. Then I rushed out, just before closing time, to get some supper. Bought Polish bread, a lettuce, some brie and a bottle of Castel Garcia! Bit extravagant; but it looks as if we're going to be able to afford it! . . . There's the bell!

CHAPTER NINE

20.10.73. Up rather late after quite a session with the Doc. John Colvin dropped in. Full of the political situation. He's sure there'll be a general election within the month. I couldn't care less, I told him. 'A plague on both their houses!' I said. But I could see it was important to him. Must be, I suppose, in his job – but I was thankful it wasn't mine! He's a decent chap though. Wanted to know what I thought about the chances of a cease-fire in the Middle East. As if I knew! He said he was praying the Israelis didn't get a clear victory. 'What we need is a stalemate,' he said, 'a draw. Then both sides can claim they've won and compromise.'

'D'you believe in compromise?' I asked him.

'Not much. But what can we do? Compromise and expediency rule the world today. Until we can find new principles, new morals that are really valid – I mean that people will adhere to – we all have just to carry on bodging things up as best we can. There's no other way.'

I was surprised he was so thoughtful. Can't be easy in the whirl of a big daily. But there's something steady and decent about him. Reliable. Wish I was!

The Doc rang the bell at 7.30. Bang on time. He was evidently keen as mustard. So I gave him the MS to read while I got supper. To my surprise, he was quite overcome, moved by it. I'd thought that a professional in that field might have been a bit cynical, subjected it all to clinical examination, stumbled over the commas. But not a bit. He wouldn't even talk about it at first. All through supper he hardly said a word, as if he were thinking hard.

I found no difficulty in falling in with his mood. Living so much alone, I'm used to silence. I rather like it. So our conversation was down to 'Salad?', 'Cheese?', 'Another glass of wine?', 'Coffee?' and so on. But it was an easy silence. For somebody so talkative, whose ideas seemed to bubble out of him, I found it a mark of character that he could keep his mouth shut. It wasn't until we'd finished and washed up – at which he insisted on helping me – that I felt it was time to talk.

'Well, what d'you think of our new gospel?' I asked him.

'I'm overwhelmed by it, Jude. I really am. It's years since anything's moved me so much. Greg's absolutely right. It's sensational – and I've an idea the sensation isn't going to be all that pleasant either.'

'Why?'

'Because people hold very firm beliefs – if they hold any at all – and this is going to shake them. Judas has been the scapegoat of Christianity for two millenia. The whole Crucifixion is blamed on him. His name has become a universal symbol for traitors. It's very convenient. You see the idea that we can't live up to the ideals of purity and goodness that Jesus taught, is something we don't like to face. 'Each man kills the thing he loves' – we can't really accept that. It's too humiliating, too difficult. Judas gives us all an 'out'. *We* would never have done such a thing, *he* did. So we're all right and can continue to feel virtuous. And, of course, the traitor, the informer, is a basic ingredient in every good story. It provides the drama, the contrast. There's always somebody to give the hero away. It's a symbol of our own inner contradictions, if you see what I mean.'

'But the teaching of Jesus doesn't depend on Judas, good or bad.'

'Certainly not. But it's what we were saying in Israel, remember? The doctrine is unassailable, but the life is a different matter. And people get them muddled. So now, if we accept this new version as being authentic – and I don't see how we can avoid it – it's the only contemporary document we have, a hundred and fifty years earlier than any other gospel. It's a very serious challenge to the conventional point of view – to the established church, that is. I doubt if they'll be able to accept it. Think what it means! The traitor turns out to be the hero! A complete *volte face*. How's the Pope, who can't be wrong, going to swallow that? Right at the climax, in the heart of the Passion! It'll set the entire Ecumenical Council whirling like dervishes! And –' the Doc burst out into that infectious laugh of his, '... that is something I should really like to see! Excuse my irreverence,' he went on, 'but, being on the sidelines, a mere student of religion, not an exponent, I tend to be a bit detached. I look for truth, not dogma – and this thing has an unmistakable ring of truth to it. There are tiny indications in the Gospels – left in by mistake, maybe – we are told that Judas 'carried the bag', that is, he looked after the money. He was the administrator, so to speak, the practical apostle whom Jesus relied upon. This much is known, though it's so casually mentioned nobody has given it much thought. But now it fits. We see he was the closest, most beloved of the disciples, who gave up his own part in that magical Last Supper so that Jesus might have time to finish what had to be done, undisturbed.'

The Doc paused, thoughtful. 'You see,' he went on after a moment, 'I think there may have been a miscalculation.'

'A miscalculation?' I didn't follow.

'Yes. Only a few days before, at Ephraim, Jesus was telling His disciples, "My time is not yet." As if, perhaps, He hadn't realized the ominous situation growing in Jerusalem. Then in the way things do, the whole tempo had quickened. Suddenly there was no time. Before it might have been a matter of weeks, now it was a matter of hours before His inevitable end. And He still had things to say, necessary, secret, sacred things that He had held back until He was certain His disciples were ready to receive them. But He needed time – and now, suddenly, there was no time! Imagine how the tensions must have been building! The adulation of the people, wanting to crown Him King! The hatred of the priests! – and they had no time either! They must get Him before the Passover. And it had to be done secretly. If the people got wind of what they were up to, there could be riots and that would set the Roman legions off. No wonder it's called the Passion! Whew!'

I could see the Doctor enjoyed the drama of it. His eyes were positively dancing with excitement. It was all vividly real to him.

'On either side things had to be done quickly. So Jesus made His extraordinary decision. He saw that the only possibility for them to reach the stillness necessary to give them their final needs must be after His death, when the horror of the Crucifixion was over. They must have known of the ritual; but they had to partake of the communion together, the actual sharing of what we have come to know as the Last Supper. They had to know how to create that thread you talked about – remember? – that connection between Him and them and to do it they had to share His flesh and blood; but beyond this, they had to know how to reach that special level of being in which they could bring Him back, rematerialize Him, to give them the strength to carry their faith into life without Him. So the resurrection was essential – and to make all the preparations for something that we can only call magic, He had only an hour or two!'

The Doc paused again as if to let the drama of the whole thing sink in.

'It all turned on whether Judas could gain that much time. The resurrection depended upon it. And he accepted the responsibility. It was a priceless gift – if he could bring it off – and of course he was equal to it. He was a man of the world – Iscariot means 'of the city' – not a simple man, a fisherman. Besides he had connections, through his father, with the establishment. And, above all, he had the guts! When the guards found he was fooling them, they could easily have killed him and thrown him in the nearest ditch. Nobody would have blamed them. Emotions were running very high. To them, if he didn't deliver, he certainly was a traitor!'

As usual, the picture he painted was vivid. But he had not finished. 'Judas, it seems now, understood more deeply than the others. He had accepted, as none of them had, that Jesus meant what He said. His hour was come. There was nothing to be done. Sooner or later, they would get Him – and He was quite prepared for it. All Judas had to do was to gain time – two hours, three hours – and he did it. It was a piece of real self-effacing heroism – and the proof of the value Jesus placed on it is there! His last act as a free man, was to take him in His arms and declare him a saint. Instead of which he has been vilified ever since! It's a fantastic paradox!'

'How on earth did it get into the Gospels?' I asked.

'Ah! That's the real mystery, the sinister machiavellian influence at work behind the whole thing. But, after all, what we have been previously told to believe is an impossible contradiction. Here is Jesus who, by any standards, was an extraordinary being. He had unique powers of healing, He breathed compassion and love, He is described as being one "to whom all things are known", how could He possibly have been ignorant of Judas' character – if he had such a character – how could He possibly have permitted an arch traitor to be privy to His closest intimacy? It is simply unbelievable. It can't be true. I never did believe it. So this new light on it all is a tremendous satisfaction to me, personally. But that's by the way. Here, at last, is proof of Jesus' stature as a *man*. He wasn't a naive simpleton, duped by His closest followers, a sort of holy fool. How people have swallowed such a thing all these centuries, beats me!'

'But how,' I asked him, 'could such a story possibly arise? Who could have believed it in the first place?'

'I haven't the least idea. But we must remember there were many forces at work. It was one of the turning points of history. Everything was in the melting pot in that part of the world. There were all sorts of sects, fanatical sects – like those Qumran people – all of them had revelations, all of them were striving for recognition, for adherents, and so on. A rival sect might have done it.'

'Written it into the gospels, you mean?'

'Exactly. To belittle the Jesus sect, to suggest that if He was such a simpleton as to have a traitor close to Him and not know it, He must have been a very "unevolved" person. So all He stood for must be worthless.'

'It's pretty subtle,' I said.

'But luckily it didn't work.'

'The high priest's lot might have done it. Infiltrated the movement, so to speak.'

'They might. Something of the kind must have happened. After all, nothing is recorded, none of the gospels were written down, as far as we know, for at least a hundred years. That's a long time. But there may have been manuscripts, like this one, kicking around. Unscrupulous hands might have had access to them. Who knows? If you read the gospels you can't help feeling a good deal of cobbling has gone on. There are passages which don't seem to follow on what went before, which jump, so to speak. Verses seem to have been inserted here and there. There are things which don't feel right, as if they had been added to, or altered. In this new version of ours the sequence is quite different. There are lines that turn up and sound all right; but I think, from memory, that if you compare them with the other gospels, you'll find the same thing, almost word for word, but in quite a different context, so which is right? Anything may have happened. It's all extraordinary. Quite extraordinary.'

I could see the Doc was getting a big kick out of the whole thing. It was right up his street. Now he lapsed into silence, staring across the room, all sorts of erudite points turning in his head I suspect, which would have been quite lost on me. For some minutes my mind had been taking quite a different direction. 'I can't help comparing it with that ritual you saw in the Temple in China,' I said.

'Ah! I wondered if you'd notice it. The same thing, I'm sure. That threadlike connection you spoke about. Yes. The Chinese ritual may have been a bit lower grade, so to speak, but the principle is identical. Must be.' He paused again, reflective, 'You know, I think the possibility of resurrection or rematerialization has always been known to people who have reached a certain level in their evolution, and it seems the Last Supper and that ceremony I saw in China are examples of it. But –' and the Doc turned to me and I saw his face glowing with a sort of wonder. He was evidently quite uplifted, moved, at having seen something he had never seen before, 'what makes it so wonderful, far more wonderful, for me, than it ever was before, is that it wasn't something that Jesus did *alone* – a sort of magical demonstration of His powers – like His ability to heal – it was *something the disciples did*. He opened the possibility for them, by actually entering into them with His flesh and blood, but they, out of their need and love, brought Him back to them. I find this participation a deeply moving human parable in itself. The higher powers are not on quite another level, impossible of access, they are within our reach. If our need is great enough, we – ordinary beings like you and me – can call on them to help us. Of course we have to admit the disciples weren't 'ordinary'. They were picked by Jesus because He saw their possibilities. They could be taught. But essentially, they were men, human beings; so other men, all men, can identify with them. I never saw that until you put this translation in my hand. It's come as a sort of revelation to me. Peter's terrible cry: "Have mercy on our loneliness" can always be answered.'

The Doc paused again and I could feel another knot of thoughts tying in his head, but these things didn't excite me as they did him. Judas I could understand, his motives, his courage, they were clear; but the resurrection – that was a bit too much for me.

'The church has completely missed the point!' the Doc burst out again. 'How did they cook up the idea of the resurrection of the body – everybody's body – just because Jesus came back, after death, in the body – as it appeared. He was very far from being 'everybody'. And they went nap on it! It became an article of faith. It's in the Creed! It's an extraordinary piece of wishful thinking. How could they have played on the naivety and credulity of simple people in such an irresponsible way? I can't see how they arrived at it. There's no justification for it whatever in the Gospels. The whole idea of "heaven", as the human destination in some after life, is completely vague. It's never been thought out. It doesn't stand up to examination. No. Give me Buddhism every time! Reincarnation of the essence in another body on earth is a far more acceptable concept!'

I told him all this was a bit too hypothetical for me. I couldn't really follow him. 'But why,' I asked him, 'if it was like the Judas version says, was the blood and flesh watered down so to speak, to bread and wine?'

'Oh, I think that was absolutely right. The real thing is pretty strong stuff you know – more like a pagan rite. Many people would find it disgusting, revolting. We don't realize what the media have done for the world. We've been given such a wide view – superficially – of the strange customs and beliefs of people that it takes a lot to shock us. But in those days people were far more simple. A mystical rite like this would have been quite incomprehensible. It would have put people off. And the object of the Gospels, after all, was to spread the teaching of Jesus. Communion enables people to partake allegorically, at a remove, in that sacred supper. It helps them. Imagine what would have happened if the real thing had been known! Zealots would have been cutting themselves up all over the place! Christianity could never have survived it.'

85

'I must say,' I said, 'I do find it all a bit queer. Too much for an ordinary man, like myself.'

'Yes, I agree. It belongs to that part of reality we tend to think of as unreality because we can't grasp it. That's why I think the publication of a thing like this will cause quite a stir.'

I got up. 'That reminds me,' I said, 'I've done a mosaic of the photos.' And I showed it him.

'Very impressive,' he said, as he examined it. 'What it is to be a professional! Will you put it in your book?'

I told him that was the idea. 'I'd like to have your advice,' I said, 'about layout, comment, and so on. Could we meet in a day or two when I've worked the thing out a bit more?'

Doc Ramsay said he'd be glad to do so, thanked me for supper and left.

'It's been a memorable evening,' he said.

CHAPTER TEN

21.10.73. It took me until quite late to write up the diary yesterday night after the Doc had gone and when I went to bed I found I couldn't sleep. The thing had got to me somehow. I heard that ominous beating on the door. Only Judas could meet the emergency. I saw how I'd always had a feeling of naive devotion about the disciples. They just 'worshipped' Jesus. They were puppets round the central figure, like children. But it was a life situation as well! The day to day things, where to eat, where to sleep, where to go, all this had to be cared for, looked after. The Gospels paid little attention to it. Quite rightly. They were concerned with the teaching. But life had to be lived all the same. It couldn't all be parables and miracles. Judas 'carried the bag'. He was the responsible one. He looked after things. I could see his angle ... I suppose I must have dropped off then; but I woke later in the sweat of a nightmare. Somebody had told me to go somewhere, do something. It was dangerous. It had to be done in a hurry – and I couldn't do it, couldn't face it. I tried to get away. I was struggling to get away ... I woke in the struggle. It was an enormous relief. I didn't have to face anything. I needn't betray anybody. I was just me, safe in bed. Thank God, I thought, for anonymity!

22.10.73. Cease fire in Egypt! The Doc phoned. He was quite upset. 'Another week and Israel would have been in Cairo!' he said. He rang to tell me he was leaving town. His friends had returned, so he'd be going down to his own little place near Dorking. Would I care to come along and stay over next weekend? It was quite a small place, but he could give me a bed. He'd been having thoughts about the book, the best way to present it, and so on. We hadn't been very practical the other evening when I'd given him that excellent supper. He gave me the address: Brook Cottage, Westcott, said I could get a Green Line from Victoria – if they were still running – and take a taxi out from Dorking town. Only ten minutes. 'Come on Friday,' he said, 'I'll expect you about teatime, before it gets dark. The road's a bit muddy at this time of the year. And bring that translation along with you,' he added, 'I'd like to read through it again. I've got books there. We could compare it with the other gospels.' I said I'd look forward to it.

29.10.73. Back, after a weekend at the Doc's cottage. Got down to Dorking all right and when I gave the address to the taxi driver, he seemed to know it at once. 'That'll be Dr Ramsay's won't it, sir?' Funny how, living in town, you forget country people still know each other. 'Nice little place,' he went on as he drove, 'but damp, they say, at this time of year. Yes. His mother bought it just after the war. She passed on some years back. I was a boy then. But I remember her. Fine old lady! Ninety she was, they said, and spry, right up to the end. Very healthy, this part of the world.'

He turned off the mainroad through some gates and along a muddy lane. 'The Doctor's back from foreign parts, I hear,' he continued as we negotiated the puddles. I was amused at the way he didn't actually ask questions, but made statements which you could take as questions, if you liked. I said I believed he was. We crossed an old bridge with a waterfall beyond it and stopped. 'Here we are, sir,' said the driver, 'Brook Cottage.' I thanked him and paid him off.

The first thing I noticed was the silence after the noise of town. Yet the sound of running water was loud. But that wasn't a noise: it was peaceful. If you could hear Time passing, this is what it would sound like. I pushed the gate open and down at the end of the path stood the cottage. You couldn't see it from the road. It was a little thatched place. Streams seemed to run either side of it, as if it was on an island. Set in a cup of woods, it really looked like one of those dream cottages you see in children's story books: four windows and a door, black beams in white plaster, a porch and smoke coming out of the chimney. Ye olde worlde! It was good enough to stop me and I stood, listening to the water, looking at the glow of the lamps behind the leaded panes, and thinking how incongruous it seemed for the Doc to come home from the heat of India to a place like this. It was the last thing I'd expected, more surprising than his hideout in the Abbey even. I knocked on the door. It opened and there stood Gregory Cippico!

'Hullo!' he welcomed me, 'come on in.'

I suppose I must have stopped and stared, I was so surprised.

'How on earth did you get here?' I said.

'Flew in yesterday. Here, let me take your case.'

I followed him through into the little hall.

I slipped off my raincoat and hung it on a peg. Greg put my case against the wall. 'Uncle Jon will show you your room later, I expect. The living room's through here. Come in and warm up by the fire. It's chilly.' I followed him in.

My head almost touched the ceiling beams, heavy and black. Logs burned in an open fireplace big enough for two to sit under the chimney. At the other end of the room a wide bay window looked out over the garden. The whole room seemed to be lined with books.

'Uncle Jon's just gone to the post. He'll be back in five minutes.' Greg pulled a chair up to the fire. 'Sit down. Did you have any difficulty getting down?' I told him I had not.

'What a wonderful room!' I said. 'May I have a look round?'

'Of course.'

It was the sort of place you want to prowl about in, like a

89

cat, before you settle. I went to the window. The light had almost gone. There wasn't a sound but the water. Across the stream, a pond with reeds, a huge tree, black in the dusk, woods all round, listening. We might have been in the depths of the country, not just an hour from town.

'There's a badger set in the hillside there,' said Greg at my elbow, 'foxes too. And the deer eat all the rosebuds! Makes Uncle Jon wild!'

I said I thought it was wonderful.

'Yes. Quite a legacy. Kitty — that's Uncle Jon's old mother — bought it just after the war for a thousand pounds. Must be worth twenty today. She bred Dalmatians. Built this garden. But now Uncle Jon's going to do things to it.'

We came back towards the fire. The light shone on old tables. The books gave it a mellow, lived-in feeling.

'What a place to come back to!' I said. 'When you retire!'

Greg nodded. 'Uncle Jon's always been lucky. I feel he'll miss the sun, though . . . But,' he sighed surprisingly, 'old people like to come home to die.'

'He's not that old, surely.'

'No. He wears well, but still . . . Cigarette?'

I took one and we sat.

'I didn't write to thank you for your letter — and the translation of the scroll,' I said, 'because you were off to Israel. Did you go?'

'Yes. I went,' he answered, rather reluctantly, I thought. 'I only got back to Rome the day before yesterday. Then I came straight on here.'

'Was the trip successful?'

'I'm afraid not. Everything was pretty difficult, in fact. With the war over and yet not over, people hadn't much time to help me.'

I felt, from his tone of voice, that he thought they ought to have helped him all the same.

'It wasn't the best time,' I said.

'No, indeed. I managed to find the boy who first barged in and offered the scroll to Julia Caesar, remember?'

'That must have been difficult enough,' I said. 'Did he help?'

'No. It cost quite a lot to get him to open his mouth even.' Greg spoke with some irritation. 'And then all I managed to get out of him was that the other man – the thug – who burst in later and threatened Mrs Caesar – whom he called his brother, had gone off somewhere – in connection with the war, he said, and had buried the scroll! But where he never would say – if he knew.'

'Buried it!'

'Yes. Fatal, of course. Six feet of snow on the Golan Heights. It's probably a lump of glue by now!' and Greg threw out his hands in a gesture of frustration.

I said I was terribly disappointed for him, but, inside I couldn't help thinking that now only the photos remained – and I had them!

'My disappointment is entirely beside the point,' Greg observed in a tone of voice evidently intended to put me in my place. 'This is a loss to the world. It is a situation for which words are quite inadequate. A priceless document, unique! – And it falls into the hands of a fool!'

And Greg glared at me, as if I was responsible.

'Think of it, Jude! Think of it! We had it in our hands! We touched it! Saw it! And then we let it go! We should never have given it back. We should have –'

'But you didn't know what was on it then,' I reminded him.

'No. But a scroll, any scroll – we should have realized – I should have realized – it was bound to have value ... When I think of a thing like that! The only contemporary record of the end of our Dear Lord's life – in the hands of a fool – an ignorant fool – who won't sell it – and then buries it! Buries it!'

I think he still had a lot to say; but luckily there was the sound of heavy footsteps outside. The door burst wide open and in came the Doctor.

'Well, Jude!' he greeted me warmly. 'Glad you got down all right. Nice to have Greg here, isn't it? Quite a surprise!'

Without waiting for an answer, he swept through into the hall to hang up his coat. 'Mary!' I heard him call, 'Mary! D'you think you could manage some tea?'

There was an answer from somewhere and the Doc came back, 'Jolly lucky to have such a mild winter with all these cuts hanging over our heads.' He went to the fire and warmed his hands. 'However I've got some candles and there's a bit of wood, so whatever happens we shan't freeze!'

He bustled about, poking the fire, putting on another log, pulling out a small leaf table end and unfolding it, talking all the time, asking me how I had got down, what was the latest news on the strike, were the trains running, speculating how long society could hold together if a minority held it to ransom.

Then Mary came in with the tea tray. She was an elderly woman with a bland, genial, country face. From the way she put down the tray, you could see she'd been 'in service' all her life. Doc Ramsay introduced her.

'Mary. This is Mr Heddon – friend I met in Israel. Jude, this is my invaluable housekeeper, Mary Spriggs.'

'Good afternoon, sir,' she turned to me. Very correct and contained.

'Mr Heddon's a photographer, Mary, and if you go streaking he'll put your picture in the papers.'

'God forbid!' she replied promptly, evidently horrified. 'At my age!'

'It's a good way to keep young, Mary – so they say.'

But Mary wanted no more of such improper conversation. 'Will that be all, sir?' she asked him.

The Doc thanked her and as she went out he added, 'We'll be out for supper, Mary. Got something for yourself?'

Mary said that she had and closed the door.

After tea, when Greg had taken out the tray and we were all settled round the fire, the Doc lit his pipe and turned to me.

'I suppose Greg's told you he drew a blank in Israel?' I nodded and he went on. 'I fear that means we can say goodbye to any hope of getting our hands on the original scroll, eh, Greg?'

'It looks like it.'

'It's a pity. But I don't think it really matters. After all, four of us have seen and handled it. That's sufficient proof that it really did exist and . . .'

'And we have the photos,' I added.

'Exactly. We have everything, in fact, that we should have had if we were in possession of the scroll. We've got the message, so to speak. The pith of something entirely new and original is there. The question is the best way to make it public – if it should be made public. What do you say, Greg?'

'Anything authentic that belongs to our Lord's life, belongs to the world,' Greg answered without hesitation.

'Even if it conflicts – radically – with what we have understood previously?'

'We can't help that, can we? We shall have to learn to accommodate it, to take it into our understanding. It may be difficult; but, since it is a contemporary account – the only contemporary account – of part of our Lord's life and suffering, it isn't dependent on opinion. It isn't theory, to be argued about. There it is! It's the truth.'

'I'm glad you feel like that,' said the Doc, 'and I hope the same view will be taken by your superiors in Rome.'

'I am sure it will.'

'Are you? Well, frankly I am not. It involves explaining – and accepting – a highly esoteric ritual, which I suspect a lot of them will never have heard of, and it implies a complete *volte face* in the Church's attitude to Judas.'

'That's not so difficult.' Greg sounded perfectly confident.

'Judas acted as he did because our Lord wished it. He could not do otherwise. It's not so very different. In the version we have, he was still offered money and agreed to betray the Lord. He still finally took the guards to Gethsemane. He need not have done so. He could have kept up the wild goose chase, until Jesus had escaped, even if it had cost him his life.'

'And the eating of the flesh and drinking the blood?'

'Communion is a ritual that has been an immense consolation to tens of thousands of people who have partaken of it. They cannot share what the disciples shared; but they come as near as they can. You do not understand, Uncle Jon, the wisdom and compassion of the Church.'

'Perhaps not.' Doc Ramsay smiled non-committally, 'Well, anyhow, you see no difficulty about publication?'

'Not in the very least,' Greg rejoined.

'Jude,' the Doc turned to me, 'you're the book man. How do you suggest we go about it?'

I told them that as soon as any agent put it about that there was a property of this kind coming onto the market – papers, publishers, the media – they would all come running. 'It's only a matter of coordinating it properly.'

'And making sure,' Greg stopped me, 'that our Lord's life is presented as the sacred thing it is. We mustn't allow it to become cheap or sensational.'

'You can't prevent it being sensational, Greg, because it is. Highly sensational. Hightly controversial.'

'As an outsider,' I interrupted them, 'I don't think you can cheapen the thing itself. It's too authentic for that. All that could cheapen it would be the way we presented it.'

'How can we avoid that?'

I told them I thought we might all collaborate. 'I could write a strictly factual account of the way it happened, the thousand to one chance that I was there, the way we got the photos, the war coming and so on. Just the facts. You –' I turned to Greg, 'could pick it up from there, telling what happened in Mrs Caesar's room, how you arranged the translation when you got the photos, your return to Israel and how you drew a blank. That would lead us on to the translators. They will obviously have a lot to say about the actual script. They must have been pretty surprised . . .'

'They certainly were,' Greg put in.

'. . . and I expect they'll have a lot of technical points about the bits they've inserted, and all that.'

'That ought to go in an appendix,' said the Doc, 'it's not of interest to the general reader.'

'We could follow this with the actual photos,' I went on, 'possibly that fold-out mosaic I showed you, Doc, and then come to the actual translation . . .'

'And why not add,' Greg put in, 'a critical commentary by some of the experts; I'm sure they'd be interested. Uncle Jon, couldn't you wind it all up with some general observations: the parallels to the other gospel texts, possible corruptions, additions – all those questionable things you think so important?'

'They are important,' said the Doc, 'but I don't think I could do that. There are plenty of biblical scholars more up in all that sort of thing than I am. In any case, I think you'll need two commentators, one who's for the new version and one who's against it!'

'There's nothing like a bit of controversy,' I said.

We talked a lot more about it all. In fact for the whole weekend we didn't talk about much else! But it was really just letting off steam. We were all excited about it. We didn't take it much further.

I came back to town feeling pretty optimistic. It looks as if this really is a valuable property. The photos are the key to it all – and they're mine! I can legitimately draw a contract and take the royalties. Any other contributors can be paid off outright. There might be several thousand pounds in it! What I've alway dreamed of – a bit of a balance in the bank so I can relax and not be always running after the next book.

That would be wonderful! I could go East, look for unusual subjects in the Philippines, New Guinea . . .

I enjoyed the weekend. The Doctor's little place is a gem.

CHAPTER ELEVEN

3.11.73. Greg phoned me from Rome. He asked me to return my copy of the translation. The translators, he said, had done some more work on it and had come up with a new version. Far better. Apparently, they didn't want the old one knocking about. Professional pride and all that. I didn't really see it was necessary; but, of course, I promised to put it in the post, as he wished. Greg said he would send me over the new one in the course of a day or two. Otherwise everything was fine. He'd had some ideas for commentators, but we could talk that over when we met. I said I'd got the thing lined up my end – as far as we could go at the moment. He said he hoped to be over the following weekend and rang off.

I don't know why I didn't feel quite happy about that conversation. Something in his tone of voice – a sort of evasiveness – I couldn't really say. But I felt uneasy and I sat for quite a time wondering ... Did he want the translation back to get it out of my hands?

Suddenly I saw it didn't matter. I spent the next two hours photographing it, page by page. I developed out the negs and printed them. They were okay. Then I wrote Greg a brief note enclosing the translation. If there was anything in my hunch, I was covered. Probably ridiculous to be so suspicious. He's always been perfectly decent.

5.11.73. I was quite right. Greg's a bastard. I might have known. I have always distrusted priests. I was put onto it by Doc Ramsay. He rang me, saying he had to come to town and would I meet him at the Athenaeum for lunch.

After coffee, he told me Greg had rung him last night.

It seems his 'superiors' – and the Doc didn't really know who they were – there's a sort of mystery about all that which I don't like – anyway, these people, whoever they are, apparently want to take over the publication of the book. Their excuse is that it's so important they feel it should appear under 'official', church auspices, and not as a private publication. The Doc was quite apologetic about it. He assured me it was nothing to do with him. He was just tipping me off so that, if I heard from Greg, I should have had time to think it over and know what I wanted to say.

I told him I knew very well what I wanted to say and would say it, loud and clear. The photos were mine. I'd taken them. I held the negatives. Without the photos, no book.

'I'm a professional man,' I told him, 'and that means, besides the technical know-how, a sort of flair for being at the right place at the right time. The only reason I'm able to make a go of it at all, is this luck – if that's what it is. I seem to turn up just when the trouble occurs, or when the light is right. The scroll is a perfect example of it – a fantastic bit of luck. But my livelihood depends on it. I've no intention of letting other people climb on my back and ride that luck – or squeeze me out. I'm not a hack photographer you engage at so much a shot. If Greg thinks that, well, he'd better think again.'

The Doc nodded. 'I agree. I think it's a stupid idea. All these "official" books issued by "bodies", amorphous sort of "committee" publications – they're all as dull as ditchwater. Your idea of a racy, human story, leading up to that fantastic bedroom scene – that's the way to do it. I'm dead against Greg in this.'

'Well, thank God for that, anyway!'

'But, in fairness to him,' the Doctor went on, 'I think we do have to remember he's just a backroom boy. I mean he's just a "Father", not a bishop or a cardinal. I'm sure he felt bound to tell his superiors – whoever they may be – about all this. They must have sent him back to Israel, after all. If they tell him they want to sponsor the thing, what can he do? He must obey orders. He knew it would upset you. He said so on the phone.'

'Very decent of him,' I put in – rather acidly I'm afraid.

'After all, you must admit it's pretty explosive material. To have it appear independently, when one of their own people was mixed up in it, well, it wouldn't look very good – from their point of view. They're quite intelligent enough to realize it's a delicate situation. It contradicts beliefs that have been held for centuries. Far better to put their own imprimatur on it than have some private individuals come out with it and cock snooks at them. They take themselves pretty seriously.'

'Well, anyhow,' I said, 'I'm not letting go of my photos – and that's that.'

The Doc laughed. 'I've no doubt they'll offer to pay you handsomely and star your name on the title page.'

'That's not what I want.'

'I can quite understand that.'

'So I suppose I shall hear from Greg?'

'Either that, or he'll turn up. He'll have to turn up when he knows how you feel – or invite you to Rome.'

'I've no intention of going to Rome,' I said, 'and Greg's wasting his time if he thinks he can persuade me by coming over.'

'That's the stuff! David and Goliath!' he looked at his watch and abruptly got up. 'I've got an appointment – and I'm late, as usual. Do excuse me. Let's keep in touch. I'm enjoying this. Phone me if you hear anything. I'll do the same.'

Maybe the Doc was enjoying himself, but I came home very depressed. Nothing ever seems to go smoothly for me. I have to battle every inch. I know you have to fight for success; but I never seem quite to make it. I'm always hanging on by my eyebrows. This thing would have given me quite a different position. And now? Why do I struggle? What for?

7.11.73. A letter in the post from Greg, just as the Doc thought. And more or less repeating his words. Very sorry to have to suggest a change of plan, but this 'remarkable piece of contemporary evidence of our Lord's Passion' should, we feel, be 'dignified' by appearing under 'official auspices' and so on. 'Due prominence' would be given to my 'outstanding work' for which he hoped he could persuade me to accept a fee 'commensurate with my contribution'. He felt sure I would appreciate the importance of the situation and would collaborate with the wish of his superiors to 'bless this great event' in a manner consistent with their position as 'guardians and defenders of the word of God'. Piss and wind.

I rang the Doc at once and read him the letter over the phone.

'Pretty pompous!' was his reaction. 'They sound as if they're pulling out the stops. What will you do?'

'I'm writing to Greg to tell him there's nothing doing.'

'And then?'

'Then I shall go ahead myself. I've got the photos and the translation.'

'I thought you said you'd sent it back.'

'I did – but I made a photographed copy.'

'Good for you.'

'If we want comment from an 'expert' point of view on any of the technical points, I'm sure we can easily get it.'

'Of course. That's all trimmings.' The Doc confirmed my own thoughts. 'The photos and some sort of translation are all that is necessary. If it's a bit rough, all the better. Then the pundits can busy themselves arguing and making a better one. Good publicity!'

After we'd rung off, I sat down feeling quite dead about it

all. It came back to me how when Greg had phoned me that night and asked me to photograph the scroll, I'd had a premonition. A voice inside me had said 'Don't!' I'd paid no attention. But now, my professional position, my livelihood was at stake. I sat down and wrote to Greg.

My dear Gregory Cippico,

I'm afraid I cannot agree to the suggestions made in your letter, which are, as you will realize, very different from those we discussed in the UK recently. I intend to go ahead and publish my photos with some sort of translation.

If your people would care to collaborate with me, I would, of course, be delighted. Some sort of foreword or introduction perhaps? Would His Holiness care to comment? Naturally anything of this kind would be of value. Nevertheless the interest lies in the photos and text, as I think you will agree.

Sincerely, etc.

Writing this gave me a sudden excess of energy. I decided to make extracts from this diary. I calculated that 10,000 words would be enough to set the scene and give detail of the incidents leading up to my part in it.

9.11.73. Two days on my intro: It's come out all right. Interesting and quite vivid, I think. Factual, straightforward, just an easy-to-read account of it all.

Phoned the Doc about using Greg's translation. He thought it would be better to get another one done. If they wanted to be difficult and claim copyright infringement, it could lead to having to withdraw the book. 'But there's no difficulty about a translation. Leave it to me. I'll ring round and give you a name.'

'What about commentators?'

'Leave it for a day or two. It might be better without.'

Now I've decided to go ahead, I don't want to waste any

time. Must get it all in my agent's hands by the end of next week.

Later. The Doc called back and gave me two possibilities for translators. 'Did I know Greg was over again?' he added. I was surprised. I told him, no. 'I think he's a bit wound up about the whole thing,' the Doc observed. I told him, so was I! He said he was sure he'd ring me – There's the phone . . .

10.11.73. What a conversation! When I lifted the phone, it was, of course, Greg. Could he come round and see me? I said, Certainly; but if it had anything to do with the book, he must know that I wouldn't change my position. All the same, he said, he'd like to have a chat. I told him how to get to me and he asked if he could come right over. I said I'd be glad to see him any time.

So, in a quarter of an hour the bell rang. He came in, making an obvious effort to be affable, admired my room – even the view of the Victoria and Albert over the roofs! – and it wasn't long before he came to the point.

He started off by excusing himself. This new move was nothing to do with him, personally. He seemed very anxious I should understand that. I probably realized, he said, that taking Holy Orders meant being under orders. As he had just happened to be mixed up in this affair, his superiors – I hated that word 'superiors' – who is superior? – had, quite naturally, asked him to undertake the job of arranging publication in the way that seemed, to them, best.

'It doesn't seem best to me,' I said.

'Jude,' he said, 'excuse me; but I take it you're not a religious man – in the technical sense of the word – I mean your life is not devoted to the service of Our Lord?'

'No.' I found it made me bristle. 'It's not.'

'So, to you, this whole incident is just a lucky chance out of which, quite normally, you expect to make some money?'

'Why not? It's my profession.'

'Quite. So perhaps it's a little difficult for you to

understand how important all this is to us. That scroll was a priceless relic. Perhaps more sacred than anything in christendom. It must have been written by someone in the very heart of the life of Jesus. How else could he have known such things? Perhaps it was penned, in that desolate wilderness, by Judas himself. Perhaps, since he may have been an educated man, he understood he had a duty to bear witness, not just by his life, but in some way beyond his life, to generations to come, what Jesus had been to him, how He had taught, died and returned to them all ... Well, now, your photos, the translation, is all that is left. It is tragic. But the little that remains is infinitely precious to us ...'

He broke off, and I could see he was really moved. After clearing his throat, he went on, 'I happened to get mixed up in all this, just as you did, by pure luck. I happened to have a hunch, as they say, that we ought to get a record of the thing. It was extraordinarily fortunate for us – and perhaps for the world – that we were able, thanks to you, to do so.' He broke off and when he spoke again his voice had taken on that 'holy' note that always gets me. 'I too have my small part in this. Are we not all instruments in a design which far transcends our personal role in it? I am asking you to try to understand that. Because of my calling, I am most anxious that all this should be brought to its sacred fruition under the aegis of the Church.'

There was something sententious in the way he spoke. Mealy mouthed. I didn't believe him. There was something going on. I didn't know what it was but I wasn't going to fall for it. So, I told him I was sure he would be glad to get his hands on my photos, but ...

'Oh, please!' he cut in, 'try not to think of it like that.'

'But,' I went on, 'you also have to understand that nobody but a professional, with the right cameras and lenses, with the right know how and experience, could possibly have got those shots in such circumstances. Without me there would be no record of anything. I think I have a perfect right to publish my own work.'

'Of course. Nobody would dream of belittling your work and your right to it. But the circumstances are very special and that is why I am pleading with you to allow us this privilege. Naturally we should pay the highest tribute to your skills and your prompt cooperation in what was, after all, a most unusual situation. It was remarkable, truly remarkable. Also, if it interests you, we would hope to reimburse you handsomely for your negatives – that would be the very least we could do.'

Ah, now, I thought, we're coming to it. But I said nothing and he went on: 'I don't want to intrude into your private affairs in any way; but what would you expect to make out of a publication such as this? I mean what would you pocket, net, after deducting agent's fees, taxation and so forth?'

I told him I had no idea. It depended on how the book sold. 'Religious subjects may seem very important to you,' I said, 'but today people aren't particularly religious. Apart from that, it isn't entirely a question of money. This is the sort of thing that will do something for my reputation, my prestige, and . . .'

'But why,' he cut in, 'if you'll excuse me, should it do any less for your career, if your name appears – very prominently – in a book published by someone else?'

I saw that, logically, what he said was right; but somehow the man made me stubborn. Egoism, I suppose. I wanted to do it myself.

'Sorry,' I said; 'but I happen to think it would.'

'Let's be frank, Jude.' He was getting a bit shorter now. Harder. 'Prestige, position, and all the rest of it, they're all very well, but finally what sets us all free to do what we want, is cash. Supposing I were to offer you two thousand pounds, as a free gift, in cash, so that no question of taxation arose, would that interest you at all?'

'Not a bit,' I said. 'I never sell my work outright. I always sell on a royalty basis.'

'I'm afraid I'm not up in the technicalities of these things, but I'm sure we could arrange participation on some royalty basis – in addition to the cash sum – but I'd have to talk it over with my people. Some figure like 20 per cent of the gross sales, perhaps. You see we aren't commercial. We don't want to make any money out of it ourselves –' That doesn't sound like the Church, I thought, from what I know of it. But he was going on. 'Our motives are, as I hope I've explained, concerned with,' he hesitated, 'with "fitness", what we think ought to be done, with altruism, if you will – a sort of spiritual obligation to Christians everywhere.'

I knew that 20 per cent of the gross was very high. Far beyond what 'illustrations' would naturally attract. Of course these were different; but I began to detect a certain anxiety on his part to conclude the deal. If he would go this far, he would probably go farther ... Anyway I didn't feel like letting the thing out of my hands.

'I don't see it like that,' I said, getting up. 'I'm attached to my own work, jealous of it, if you like. So I'm afraid you'll have to resign yourself to publishing through me, if you want to publish at all ...'

'Of course we want to publish,' he put in quickly.

'Well, as I said in my letter, if you care to let me have anything you want to say, relevant to it all, I'll be glad to put it in. After all,' I added, a little shortly I suppose, for I was sick of the conversation, 'it makes no difference, as far as I can see, whether you publish or I do. I'm not going to cheapen the thing, to denigrate it in any way. I'm as aware as you are of the importance of it. I know it's serious. I'll even let you see the proofs – provided you don't hold them up. I expect to have it all in the publisher's hands within a fortnight.'

He sat there staring at me for a moment. Then he got up too. 'It's very sad,' he said, 'to see a man putting his personal pride, his personal ambition first — in a thing so big, so sacred, as this. You'll think I'm preaching if I say it's serious for you. But it is, Jude; it is serious — and one day, perhaps, you'll see it.'

That made me very angry. 'If it's a question of my pride and ambition against yours,' I retorted, 'presumably as you represent the Church, yours is a good deal larger!'

'I'm sorry we have to part like this,' he said at the door.

I shrugged. 'Well, that's the way it is. Goodnight!'

It's taken me quite a time to quiet down, now he's gone. Serious for me! What damned cheek! No wonder the churches are empty! I've just got out my introduction and read it again. There isn't anything in it that anyone could possibly object to. I feel perfectly justified. And, as for the money, well the book might make more than that. You never know.

CHAPTER TWELVE

13.11.73. Back after a weekend down at Doc Ramsay's cottage. It has a wonderful atmosphere and I must say the more I see of him the more I like him. For all his learning and experience, he seems to me a simple man. He's the only man I ever met whom I can speak to about serious things. I feel I can trust his views about religion. I feel he could be a friend. It's rare for me to feel things like that.

When I tried to say something about all this to him, as we pulled our chairs up to the fire on Saturday evening after I arrived, he nodded and relit his pipe – it was always going out!

'It's a question of vibrations, I think, don't you? When I first met you I knew we should "get on" as they say. I felt an immediate sympathy between us which couldn't be accounted for by anything I knew about you – because I knew nothing about you! But there it was, all the same.'

'Places sometimes have the same effect, don't you think? This place, for instance!'

'Yes. I'm glad you feel it. My mother lived – and died – here. The house has a good history. You can feel it. Simple people have lived here. Good people. There's never been anything bad here. No ghosts. It's a happy place.'

'Greg's got strange vibrations,' I mused.

'Yes. Uneven. You have to keep him on the right wavelength, so to speak. You find him difficult?'

I said that I did. I didn't trust him – and I told him about his last visit, his offer and the way the conversation had gone.

'Mm.' He pressed the tobacco into the bowl, thoughtfully. 'I wonder,' he said at last.

'What?'

'If they dare.'

'Dare what?'

'Publish. I didn't want to say anything about it until you mentioned it, but Greg came down here after he left you and told me you intended to go ahead. I think he's pretty unhappy about it. He's gone back to Rome. I fancy there's some very hard thinking going on there.'

'Why?'

'Well, when it comes to the crunch, what are they getting into? Supposing they did succeed in making some arrangement with you, got you to agree to their taking on publication, what then? They'd have made themselves responsible for it, given it their blessing. It's all very well for them to say that it's something that comes within their domain; but that cuts both ways. It may end up with them having to do a lot of explaining – and very awkward at that.'

'Is it really so difficult?' I said. 'I've been thinking. Four Gospels say Judas was a traitor; one says he wasn't. Four to one. They can simply repudiate it.'

'Then they mustn't publish it,' the Doc came back at once. 'I told Greg as much. The trouble is that it's pretty powerful, pretty convincing, even if it is a minority.'

'And it's contemporary,' I reminded him.

'Yes, and that gives it an enormous pull. One thing I'm sure of, they must be wishing the thing had never turned up. Greg was mighty quick off the mark, getting you to photograph it – zeal can be a very troublesome quality sometimes.'

'Then you think they might have second thoughts?'

'Well, it would leave them free to repudiate it if they thought that was the best course. I don't think it would make much difference in the long run. My hunch is what they'd like best would be to suppress the whole thing, forget it.'

'Not while I'm around.'

'No. Besides there are such things as obligations.'

'Yes. And mine are to myself – have to be.'

'Of course. It comes back to that. But, beyond it, there's a wider question – in a thing like this. Here's something which, as Greg said, belongs to the world. That carries obligations. One can't imagine responsible people deliberately suppressing it, hiding it, losing it or selling it. That would be a real betrayal! It's impossible. They must go through with it, in some way or other.'

'Isn't it extraordinary how religious things stir people up?'

'Yes. We don't know how much we feel about these things, until they're challenged.'

The Doc put down his pipe. (It had gone out again.) He yawned and ran his fingers through his hair. 'Shall we have a drink? I picked up a bottle of Drambuie on the plane. It's not strictly a pre-prandial beverage; but if you wouldn't mind waiving the protocol, we might try it.'

I said I wouldn't mind at all and we sipped away together. It was very good. The Doc sighed as he put down his empty glass. 'I often think the monks had the right idea when they relieved the rigours of monastic life by inventing liqueurs. We've a lot to thank them for. A little tot on your way to Heaven . . . They were really holy men. They understood the one important thing.'

'And what was that?'

'That they knew nothing. It's a very important point to reach. I think it's only when you begin to approach the end of life that you realize it. Look at me. I'm accounted quite an authority in certain fields. I've spent my life studying and lecturing and teaching various aspects of religious beliefs. I know quite a lot about the Vedas; I've done a translation of the Gita; my lectures on Zen have been translated, even into Japanese. I used to think that all this would bring me finally to the heart of the matter, that I should reach a point where I should really *know*. But I see now it was all exterior, from the outside. It's like a man being expert in all the details of the design of a racing car, without ever having been at the wheel. Masses of information; but no knowledge – it's a very different thing, I see it now. Perhaps some of those monks got to the same point and decided that they and thousands like them – needed a little drink!'

We laughed. I told him I'd grown up with a positive antagonism to it all. My father had been a Baptist Deacon and I'd had religion so much rammed down my throat as a kid that I'd been very careful to keep well clear of it since.

'Yes. People do – until things go bad on them, or get serious – or dangerous. "The devil was sick, the devil a monk would be." Millions of men have spent their lives affirming or denying, acclaiming or protesting their beliefs in this, that and the other and then, suddenly; there's death! They have to face extinction. Then it looks different. It's the end.'

'Is that really true? I wonder?'

'Such as we are, ordinary men, there's no answer. We're confronted with a mystery. And the more you study it – and I've studied it for fifty years – the more mysterious it becomes. But I'm equally sure that, *at another level*' – and he laid great emphasis on the words – 'there is an answer. Only I've never reached that level, so I don't know it. When I was reading those bits in that translation of ours, the fragments after the resurrection, I saw how desperately the disciples needed Jesus back. They wanted this very same answer. He was free of His own mortality, free of death. But they were not. They hoped, so it seemed to me, that when they called Him back, now He was dead, He would give it to them. And what was the answer, there by the fire on the edge of the sea – how extraordinarily allegorical it becomes! – it's better in St John – "Feed my sheep. Feed my lambs". That sums it all up. Three words. That's the final statement, the final message. Utterly simple – and quite incomprehensible.'

He suddenly sat up and poked at the fire and remained there staring into it for a long moment. Then he relaxed back to his old position. 'Remember how you asked me what were the questions and answers between those Chinese priests and their Abbot and I said that, even if we had a transcript, it wouldn't mean anything? This is just the same. In the Gospels there is this answer – but it takes us no further. What is the food and how do you feed it? Something must pass between the shepherd and his sheep. Not words. Not explanations. Some food, some elixir of life, must give them certainty that He knows the way and will lead them home . . .'

He tailed off and sat gazing into the fire. I realized that, in a way, he wasn't speaking to me, but to himself. It was a reverie. I felt an immense sympathy for him, for it seemed to me I had exactly the same problems. At the end of an active and distinguished career, he found himself nowhere. He was lost. I often feel just the same, though I'm not at the end of my life, when these black moods of depression get me. There's no point in anything. Nothing is worthwhile. Everything will fail. There's no answer, outside or inside . . .

It was next morning when we were walking in the woods that the Doctor suddenly turned to me and said, 'Have you some project, some important project, in mind?'

I told him I had ideas, possibilities, but nothing certain.

'A man ought to have some sort of aim, something to work towards. It can be a beacon, a milestone in life. If you reach it, there's a sense of accomplishment. It's a monument you can measure yourself by. Without it, life meanders on without much point.'

I told him then of an idea that had been growing in my mind, partly as a result of his influence, of all these conversations. It was of making a symposium, a photographic symposium, to be called 'Images of God'. I thought it might be interesting to bring together such images, masterpieces, from different epochs, different locations, of how men had conceived the image of divinity. 'But of course,' I added, 'it's quite out of my reach. It would need a lot of time, a lot of money, travel, research. It's something one does when one's rich. It's not commercial – unfortunately.'

'It's a good idea.' The Doc sounded quite keen. 'Don't drop it. If you want anything enough, I am quite sure you can always get it. It seems impossible; but in some mysterious way, the possibility opens. Believe it will work, and it will!'

It was just before I was leaving that the phone rang. The Doc went into the hall to answer it. There was some conversation I didn't hear and then he called out to me that it was Greg speaking from Rome. 'He wants to see you.'

'Tell him I'm not changing my mind,' I called back. The Doc spoke and then called again: 'He says he's got another proposal to put to you.'

'All right,' I said, 'when?'

The conversation continued for a bit and then I heard the Doc ring off. He came back. 'He's coming over tomorrow and he'll ring you.'

'I wonder what it is this time?' I mused.

'I wonder.' The Doc was thoughtful too. 'Anyway, he'll probably be in touch with me. If I get wind of anything, I'll tip you off.' He looked at his watch. 'We must go or you'll miss your bus.'

'If I can get on it!'

I couldn't. There was a long queue. I didn't get back until midnight.

CHAPTER THIRTEEN

14.11.73. I thought it might be a bit awkward meeting Greg again. We hadn't parted on the best of terms. But when he called me yesterday, Monday, from Heathrow, he sounded as affable and cheerful as ever. He asked if he could come right along to see me and turned up about an hour later. I'd already made up my mind that I wouldn't give way whatever he proposed; but I suppose I was a bit edgy and on guard when I opened the door.

He was very suave and easy, inquiring after my health, how I had enjoyed my weekend with Uncle Jon, wanting to know the latest on the strikes and so on. I took his coat and I rather admired the way he sat down with a businesslike air and came straight to the point.

'Jude,' he said, 'I've been having further discussions with my people in Rome about this business and the upshot of it is that I'm going to ask you to reconsider your position.'

'I'm afraid it's too late for that now,' I told him, 'my plans are all made and . . .'

'Just a minute,' he stopped me. 'Let me tell you what I've come to say. I realize how important all this has become for you, the value you put on your work and so on. I, personally, have a good deal of sympathy for your point of view. I know the effort and ingenuity that went into getting those shots. However my people are still as determined as ever that publication ought to be "official", as they call it, so I've been instructed to make you a further offer for the outright purchase of all your rights in those negatives.'

'How much?' I said it bluntly. Mentally I had already refused it.

'Thirty thousand pounds.' He came out with it flat. The size of the sum staggered me. I didn't know what to say.

'That's a lot of money,' was all I could manage.

Greg looked me squarely in the eye and I could see he knew he'd shaken me.

'It *is* a lot of money. But, as I said last time I was here, we're not commercial and we know how to be generous. In addition I should add that we can arrange to pay you the money here, in the UK, in cash and, although it may be against the regulations, I see no reason why it should attract tax. There's only one proviso . . .' he reached for his brief case and opened it.

'And what's that?' I asked. I was still a bit paralysed mentally at the size of the sum.

'This,' he said and handed me a sheet of paper.

It had my address at the top and what followed was short and formal. It simply said in more or less legal language that in return for the sum received (which was not named) I renounced all rights in the negatives and prints of a certain 'antique document photographed by you on the night of October 5th in Israel', that I had handed them over complete and that no more remained in my possession. A second paragraph gave an undertaking that I would not write, speak or otherwise make public anything concerning the incident or my part in it for the next five years.

I stared at the paper, trying to make up my mind what to say. 'In other words,' I tried to appear judicial, 'you want an outright sale and you want me to forget all about it?'

'That's it,' said Greg, 'what do you say?'

I didn't know what to say. I suppose I was still a bit stunned.

'Well – I'd like to think it over.'

'Of course.'

'You see,' I excused myself, 'I've started things, talked to my agent in general terms, contacted a translator, and . . .'

'A couple of phone calls will fix that.' Greg was prompt

and practical. 'It's quite usual for people to change their plans or decide to handle things in another way. The less people know about all this the better. Have you sent photos to your translator?'

I told him I had not.

'Good. Don't send them – until you've decided.'

I had already decided inside. And he knew it. I was only saving my face by pretending to think things over. I'm not very good at poker. So I smiled.

'I'll consider it – carefully,' I said.

'I think you'd be very wise to do so. It isn't the sort of money that turns up every day. But I don't want to hurry you in any way.'

'When do you want an answer?'

'Suppose I call you tomorrow morning,' he said, 'then, if you've decided, I can come round and we'll conclude the deal. Shall I leave the paper for you to look over?'

I thanked him and said I should like to. He got up without more ado and moved to the door.

'If I call you about 10 o'clock, will that be too early?'

I assured him I was up long before that. 'Suits me fine,' I said. I helped him on with his coat. 'Tomorrow at ten,' he repeated as I opened the door. I said 'Okay,' to his back. He didn't waste much time, I reflected, closing the door. It was strictly business. The affability was pretty thin.

But, of course, inside, I was wildly excited. I paced up and down and made myself some coffee, my head whirling at the thought of the money. Thirty thousand pounds! It wasn't possible. That sort of sum meant freedom for life! I could invest it and, at present rates ... And all for a dozen photographs! It was ridiculous. Marvellous! Only a bestseller both sides of the Atlantic would make that sort of money. Taxed, it would be half, less than half ... What had the Doc said, only yesterday? 'If you want a thing enough, the way will open.' Extraordinary! The very next day! Here it was. I could do anything I liked! I was free! And that paper. What did it amount to? Simply an outright sale. They could use the photos without my name if they wanted to. But what did that matter? That sort of photography wasn't my line of country. It meant nothing to me, professionally. It wouldn't enhance my reputation . . . It was a hell of a price to pay for a dozen photographs. They couldn't possibly be worth it. It was mad – but that was their business . . . Why did they care so much? I shook my head. I couldn't make it out. I picked up the paper and read it again. Why should I want to speak or write about it? Did they want to cover themselves against my cutting in on their promotion? I certainly wouldn't dream of spoiling their fun – not at that figure! Thirty thousand pounds!

I went on sipping my coffee. *Father* Gregory! Funny how the man had changed. In Israel, he'd seemed just a rather dry, intellectual type, amateur archaeologist, biblical scholar perhaps, harmless, not unpleasant, very intelligent. Now he'd turned into a sort of tycoon. Very smooth. Quite at home in financial matters. Come to think of it, there were signs in Israel. All that about the Church having to pay its way. And hoping to touch that Caesar woman for a sizeable sum! Julia Caesar! I wonder what happened to her? I wonder if she stopped that cheque! Was she behind this? After all, for the Church to cough up a sum like this, it was odd. Had she put him onto it? Agreed to pay me out and sponsor it herself? It was possible. Just. The Doc had said something about her being in Rome . . . She might have thought it a way to pay me out for not performing that afternoon . . . Bit expensive! But I suppose, if you had the money . . . The money! That was the thing I kept on coming back to. I wouldn't have to worry. I could do my 'Images of God'. I could travel. All sorts of subjects would turn up. I'd let the flat. Be away a year. Take it easy. Enjoy myself . . .

I got the negs out of my deed box, looked through them, numbered the envelopes. Then I went into the darkroom. The rest of the roll was still hanging up. Blanks, not exposed.

I would hand it over to Greg. He would see from the numbers I wasn't holding anything back . . . I put it in the envelope with all the negs. The set of prints I was going to send to my translator I put in another. I read through the paper again and signed it. That completed the thing. Phew! What a morning!

Then I picked up the phone and rang the Doc.

'I've got news,' I said. Rather excitedly, I suppose.

'Then you've seen Greg?' he inquired.

'He's just left. It's absolutely incredible. D'you know what he's offered for those negatives?'

'Tell me.'

'Thirty thousand pounds.'

'Thirty thousand!' I heard him whistle.

'In notes. Can you believe it?'

'There must be a reason.' He wasn't quite so enthusiastic as I'd hoped. 'Any strings to it?'

'There's a paper he wants me to sign undertaking to keep my mouth shut about it for the next five years – that's all.'

'Five years! Mm . . . I wonder . . .' There was silence at the other end of the phone. Then, 'Did he give you any reason, any special reason?'

'No. Only what he said before – about wanting his people to do it, and so on. Nothing new.'

'You've agreed to take it?'

'Not finally. I said I wanted to think it over. I wanted to ask your advice. Don't you think I should accept?'

'It sounds wonderful.' He still sounded a bit doubtful.

'D'you remember how you said if you wanted anything enough you'd get it? It's a coincidence, isn't it?'

'It certainly is. Well look, Jude, Greg phoned me a few minutes back. He's coming down for the night. If there's anything behind it all, I expect he'll drop hints . . .'

'What could there be?'

'I don't know. But it's an awful lot of money. Well, we'll

have to see . . . I'll ring you tomorrow early, before he gets to you, if I find out anything.'

I was a bit disappointed at the way he'd taken it. I thanked him and rang off. Nothing could go wrong as far as I could see. I couldn't imagine Greg would make an offer like that and then change his mind. Why should he? I ought to have clinched the thing there and then . . .

John Colvin's just rung. Wants me to have a bite with him tomorrow evening. I told him I was a bit tied up and we agreed he'd call tomorrow, if he was free. He'll be pretty surprised at my news. Looking forward to telling him, in confidence, that I'm rich! He'll congratulate me, I know. He's a sympathetic man.

15.11.73. Why should I bother? Why should I care? What does it mean to me, all this talk about moral obligations, spiritual betrayals? I'm not going to let it influence me in the least. I've decided.

When the Doc rang I was having my breakfast. He told me Greg had just left and was coming straight on to me. He said he thought he'd found out the reason they'd offered so much. When I asked him what it was, he said, 'Hush money. I don't think they've any intention of publishing. They're just going to bury the whole thing in their archives.'

'Bury it.' I said, 'Why?'

'Too dangerous. Too explosive. They daren't risk it – I always wondered if they would.'

'So all this money is pure waste, as far as they're concerned.'

'Not at all. You had them in a spot. You were going ahead. Greg couldn't stop you. He saw the only chance was to offer you something that would be hard to refuse.'

'Very hard.'

'Yes. But now you know the issues involved . . .'

'What issues?'

'What we talked about last weekend. The thing is too big, too important for us to allow it to be suppressed – just for money. The idea that anyone can buy out a striking new addition to the Bible – well, that's betrayal with a vengeance, isn't it? People whose minds work like that . . . Whatever happens we mustn't allow that.'

'What do you suggest I do?' I saw everything slipping away.

'Refuse, of course. What else can you do? You can't be party to such a thing . . .' He paused when I didn't answer. 'Can you?' he added.

'No. I suppose not.'

'Well, of course it's up to you. But I can't imagine you doing it. After all, if you publish yourself, you won't make so much money perhaps, but you'll make quite a lot, quite enough, and you'll have the satisfaction of having done the right thing, the honourable thing. You'll sleep at nights – and that's such a blessing!' He lightened his tone. He didn't think I could be bought.

'Suppose,' I said, 'I accept the deal and then disclose the whole dirty business in an article . . .?'

'Double-cross them! Jude! I don't think it would get very far – quite apart from the fact that it isn't the sort of thing one can do. Without the photos you'd have no proof of anything. They'd just deny it. No. Besides it would be morally degrading. I can't see you getting into anything like that. After all, there are principles one must hang onto.'

'I don't know what to do,' I said. I supposed I sounded unconvinced.

'I expect I see things differently from you,' the Doc went on. 'I know you've always been indifferent, even antagonistic, to anything smacking of religion. But I've spent my whole life in the study of sacred literature, in what people have thought and written about, the most difficult and important things in life. So I suppose when a find like this turns up, which has the unmistakable stamp of truth on it, it's so sublime, so wonderful, the very idea of it being lost or buried – out of fear, out of purely selfish, sectarian ends – well, not many things get me worked up. But this does.'

I said nothing and I think he felt obliged to go on.

'If you want my advice as to what to do, I suggest you tax Greg with it directly. He only hinted at it broadly to me. I may have misinterpreted him. Then, if he admits it – and I think he will – you'll know what you're doing – and you can decide.'

I thanked him and said I would do something like that.

'It's a big temptation, Jude, I know.' I felt he was almost coaxing me. 'Greg's a good chap. He's only doing what he's told; but the arrogance, the iniquity, of the people who dared put him up to it, well – *he* ought to have refused, in my opinion. To be mixed up with anything like that. It's to out-Judas Judas a thousand times.'

After he'd rung off I sat for a long time, trying to get it straight in my head. What I wanted to do against what I ought to do, just for the sake of other people's opinion, all this went round and round in my head. I saw I had no principles, no feeling about it all. What did it matter to me? Religion was finished anyway. Why should I worry about betraying something I didn't give a damn about? I felt one of my moods coming on and a headache with it. I sat in a sort of blank emptiness. I would do what I wanted. I wouldn't be intimidated. Why should I be branded as Judas just because I was taking advantage of a marvellous opportunity? I resented it deeply. I resented the Doc putting it like that. I suppose I must have let it madden me for about an hour until I heard a knock at the door. I was glad Greg had come. I could take my anger out on him.

'Well,' he said, cheerful as ever, as he came in, 'I hope you've decided.'

I didn't ask him to sit down. 'You're a bloody crook,' I said.

No doubt it surprised him. He stopped and looked at me as if he'd never seen me before.

'You've no intention of publishing,' I went on.

He was still staring at me. A look of comprehension slowly came to his face. 'You've been talking with Uncle Jon,' he said.

'Why not? He's as disgusted as I am at the whole thing.'

'Is he now?' He seemed to be considering it and strolled past me into the room, uninvited. 'I should have thought he was too intelligent.'

'Too intelligent! Too decent, too honourable not to feel outraged at a conspiracy of this kind.'

'Try not to exaggerate,' he said patiently. 'If you want to know, it's quite true. We don't intend to publish – yet. Not until we've examined all the circumstances in greater detail.'

'It comes to the same thing.'

'Perhaps; but, in any case, why should it concern you? May I sit down?'

'Sit or stand, it's all the same to me,' I said. He sat, quite coolly, looking up at me. 'It concerns me,' I went on, 'because I believe in the truth of it and I want it known.'

'I admit,' he was perfectly smooth and unruffled, 'at first sight, it does seem believable; but, after long discussions with my colleagues, we've come to the conclusion that the whole thing's a fake.'

I just laughed at him. 'Fake!'

'Yes.' He was quite serious. 'Fake. You didn't see that thug that burst into Mrs Caesar's room to get the thing back. But I did. He wasn't a Bedouin. He wore European clothes. Who knows who he was? Just think it over, rationally, calmly, for a moment. Here's a very rich, very ignorant, very stupid woman. Just the sort that, if you're clever, you can take in. The thing's been carefully planned for a long time, accomplices who know enough about it have cooked up something that looks like a scroll. It's a passable imitation.

These brash Americans, what do they know? If you can sell quickly, before the thing's properly examined, it will pay off very handsomely.'

'Nonsense,' I said, 'he didn't even offer the scroll.'

'No. The kid brother pulled a fast one; but not quite fast enough. That was why the other one came barging in so angrily. He had his sights set on somebody else probably.'

'These things can't be faked,' I said. 'Anyway a half carbon will prove its authenticity.'

'A half carbon of what? The thing's disappeared. I don't for one moment believe it's lost or buried. They'll be hanging on to it until the war's over and some other rich, gullible tourist turns up. There's a lot of money in it and that's worth waiting for.'

'I don't believe a word of all this.' I was still very angry.

He looked me straight in the eye and smiled.

'Nor do I,' he said, 'but that will be our line if you, or Uncle Jon, or anyone else, lets the story out. We shall simply ridicule it as a lot of nonsense – and these will be our reasons.'

I was really staggered at the duplicity of it all.

'Thirty thousand pounds is a lot to pay for nonsense,' I said.

'I agree. It is. But that's our business. We have our reasons and, on the whole, we'd rather the thing didn't come out. It would upset people. It would be exaggerated. The papers would blow it up. Not to publish could develop into a smear on the Church. We'd rather not have that – in these difficult days. So we're just taking sensible precautions – and you happen to be on the receiving end.'

'But you'll publish later?' I suppose I was looking for an excuse.

'We might. But I don't think so. But, Jude,' – he was so persuasive – 'what does it matter to you? You're not really a religious man, are you? Questions like this don't really worry you? Why bother your head about it all? Today everybody, or almost everybody, has lost all interest in these things. It matters to us; but that's no reason for you to get involved. I'm sure Uncle Jon has influenced you. He's very enthusiastic and, of course, he simply revels in a situation like this. That's been his career and it suits his speculative nature. If the photos were his property it would be a different matter.'

'It's a matter of principle,' I argued, a bit weakly, I suppose, 'and truth.'

'I agree; but there is also expediency. Truth is all very well; but the trouble is that very few people can stand it. And this is the sort of truth it would be very difficult for people to stand. That is where we come in. It is the role of the Church to consider what's best for people. Would they be any better off with this contradictory information? We've decided they would not. It would perplex them. It would decrease faith, produce doubt. We don't think that's expedient. So we're prepared to go to some lengths to avoid it.'

He sat there, so much at his ease, so much master of the situation, so sure that the ends justified the means that, in my own inner contradictions, I didn't know what to say. He evidently saw his advantage.

'Jude,' he went on, 'there's another side to all this. Your profession. I've seen your work, your real work – not this little job you did just out of the generosity of your own nature – and it's good. You know it's good. But I feel it can't be an easy profession. There are too many people about with cameras these days, and that means competition. I imagine you're always working against time, thinking ahead, racking your brains for good subjects. Think what it would mean if you had time, if you didn't have to rush! It would make a world of difference to you. You know, when people are lucky – as you are in this case – I always think it's a sort of reward, as if it were meant in some way, to set a man free to do what it's important for him to do, to fulfil his latent talents, to let him flower, so to speak . . .'

He broke off and looked at me. It was true of course. It

was what I'd always wanted. I felt he knew he had won. But he went on, 'After all, if a man doesn't think of himself these days, he won't get very far. To refuse the thing you most want, most need, just for some altruistic ideal you don't believe in, that would be cutting off your nose to spite your face with a vengeance, wouldn't it?'

I went over to my deed box, unlocked it and got out the negatives. I handed them to him and made him count them and match them against the prints. I showed him the end of the roll with its blanks and how the numbers corresponded. I opened the envelope with the paper in it, which I'd signed, and handed it to him. He just nodded as he accepted all these things one after the other. 'There's nothing else?' he asked, 'you only exposed the one roll?'

'Only the one,' I answered.

'You haven't duplicated the negatives?'

'No. I haven't the facilities.'

'Good. Then here you are.'

He snapped open his briefcase and took out an envelope. There were three wads of notes in it. 'There are a hundred in each,' he said, 'you'd better count them.'

I took the bundle and thumbed through the paper. Hundred pound notes. I didn't believe what I was doing. I had ten thousand pounds in my hand. 'The other bundles are the same,' he said. I nodded. 'I'll take your word for it,' I said.

He closed the case and snapped the locks to. I put the notes into the envelope and then into the deed box, locked it and pushed it back under the desk where I keep it. When I turned round, he had already got up and was holding out his hand, smiling triumphantly, I thought.

'Thank you, Jude,' he said. I took his hand and he shook it warmly. It seemed somehow important. Fatal. 'I'm sure you'll never regret it,' he said.

'If I do, that's my funeral,' I said.

He laughed very easily and openly. 'Send me an invite and

I'll come to it!' Then he turned to go. 'I must be off. My plane leaves in an hour and a half. Lucky you're so near the terminal. I hope we'll meet again. So long, Jude.'

As I closed the door, I knew we never should meet again. But it didn't matter.

CHAPTER FOURTEEN

I've been reading through all I've written. I haven't faked anything. It was just like that. Have I done something so terrible? I can't see it. I've been practical. I've got the money. Why not? It's the beginning of a new life for me. But – somehow – it doesn't mean a thing. I feel dead inside. I can hear the Doc's voice, 'I can't see you doing that.' Why should it nag at me? He doesn't understand what it means to have to make a living ... I've just opened up the deed box to look at the notes. They didn't seem real. Just bits of paper ... Now I've got them, I don't seem to want them. What can I do with all that money? It'll catch me out, trip me up, somehow. It frightens me. There's the phone. It'll be the Doc. I won't answer.

I let it ring. But at last I did answer. It wasn't the Doc. It was John Colvin wanting to fix a date for lunch. I'm afraid I was very short with him. I just told him I couldn't. I'd got problems, I said. He sounded sorry, said he'd looked forward to hearing all about my trip and was very decent and friendly as he always is. I managed to say I would ring him next week and he seemed delighted. He'd look forward to it, he said, in his open cheerful voice. I felt guilty when I'd rung off. I always feel he's such a sound, reliable chap. Somebody you can talk to, confide in. I feel at my ease with him, as I do with the Doc. He's a man you could go to if you were in trouble. Now I am in trouble – but somehow I can't. I don't want to talk about it – yet. I'm sure he would be sympathetic, understanding – as if he were a close friend, though he's little more than an acquaintance really ... Everything's going round and round in my head. I must sort it out. I mustn't talk about it till I've got it clear. It's my business, my decision. I won't go crying on other people's shoulders . . . Damn the phone! There it is again.

This time it was the Doc. 'Well,' he said, 'what's happened? Has Greg gone?'

'Yes.' I could hardly answer. 'He's gone.'

'And . . .?' he left the question in the air.

I couldn't tell him.

'Well . . .?' He sounded as if he knew.

'I sold,' I said.

There was a long pause.

'Oh, Jude!' His voice sounded shocked. And sad. Terribly sad. 'Oh, Jude!' he repeated after a long pause. His voice was like an echo, a whisper. Then I heard a click. The line went dead. He had hung up.

Well, I suppose it's finished now. He's finished with me. He's gone. Greg's gone. Everybody's gone. I'm alone. So what? I've always been alone, more or less. I go my own way. Suit myself. Why not?

It often happens to me when my moods come on. When I can't face things, don't want to live really, don't want to go on. I just go to sleep. Maybe it's a sort of safety valve against cutting my throat! So I just dropped off, sitting there, in my chair. Forget the death-wish . . .

I suppose it must have been an hour or more later when I was wakened by the bell. I didn't want to see anybody. I sat there, listening, slowly waking up. I wouldn't answer. Then there was another, longer ring. So I got up. Better see what it was. I opened the door. There stood Julia Caesar!

'Hi, Jude!' she said. 'Thought I'd look you up.'

I stood there, staring at her. She was the last person I'd expected to see.

'Aren't you going to ask me in?' I wasn't quite awake still. I stood aside and she went past me into the flat. I smelt her perfume. She was well turned out, I remember thinking, as I closed the door behind her. I remembered that perfume from Israel. I saw her, stripping off, that afternoon when we'd got back from Jericho.

She was looking round the room. 'Hey, you've got a pretty nice little place here, Jude,' she said. I said nothing. Why had I let the woman in? She turned back to me. 'Well, so how've you been, kid?' She was very open and friendly and I suppose, if it hadn't been for that dreadful scene, I'd have had nothing against her.

'All right,' I said.

'All right!' she mimicked me with a broad smile. 'You British are all the same! Don't you ever let your hair down?' I didn't answer and she came closer. 'What's the matter? You look kinda funny. What's eating you, baby?'

Her voice was warm, almost affectionate. But I don't like being called baby.

'Nothing,' I said curtly. Then, because I had to say something, I inquired, 'Have you been long in London?'

'Got in a coupla days ago. Staying at the Savoy. Father Gregory gave me your address. Thought I'd just take a look to see if you was manning the barricades like it says in the papers.'

'It hasn't quite come to that yet.'

'No. I guess not. Hey, you know I really love London.' She turned away to look out of the window. 'You've got quite a view from here,' she said.

I was standing behind her. I didn't want the woman here. Why had I let her in? She leaned forward to look at something and I saw her skirt, tight over her backside, her legs, good, straight and a bit apart ... Why did a wave of emotion suddenly flood through me, overwhelming me with love and grief ... Liz had stood like that once, long, long ago. Why had I lost her? Why had I let her go?

'Jude,' she said, turning round. 'Guess what? I bought all your books!'

'Have you! I am flattered.'

'And they're good, Jude. Real good. Do they sell in the States?'

'No,' I told her. They hadn't got there yet.

'Why don't we bring 'em out there? I know one or two people . . .' She didn't finish. She seemed to be thinking. She sat easily on the arm of a chair. 'Got any Scotch?' she said.

'Certainly.' I went over and poured her a drink and, while I was at it, one for myself. Maybe it was what I needed.

'Yasu!' she raised her glass. 'That's the only word I learned in Greece!' She drank. 'Hey baby,' she went on, 'it's good to see you! Say, what happened to that old Professor what's his name?'

'Doctor Ramsay.' I told her I'd seen him.

'Y'know something. I was really scared that night. Those guys bursting into my room like that. Wow! Was I glad to get out of that goddam country!'

She was wearing a little hat and veil. I suppose she thought it would make her look younger. Now she got up and came over to me.

'Jude,' she put a hand up to my shoulder, 'I like you. You're a good guy. Listen. I got an idea. Don't get me wrong . . . I guess my life's pretty empty. I don't really go for this social stuff any more. All those guys trying to put their hands in my pockets. I'm through with it. How about us taking a trip? A real trip. Anywhere you say. We could be friends I guess, if we knew each other . . . You'd get a book out of it, maybe . . . I wouldn't get in your hair . . . What d'you say?'

Poor woman! It was pathetic really. She was grasping at straws. What did she know about me? I could see it all! Her drinking. The young pimps she'd get to lay her. And she'd pay all the bills! And I'd be kept. And in the middle of all that I'd take some snaps, write a book! Christ!

'Jude! Don't look at me like that. I'm on the level. No kidding. I just thought we could be friends . . . maybe . . .'

It was pathetic. She was hurt, of course. She turned away

129

to hide her face. It was the end of something for her, maybe. She crossed the room to look at something on the small table.

'Say,' she said brightly, and it sounded like a great effort. 'Where d'you get these masks? They're really something.'

Seeing her there. Something in her pose. And Liz came back again. Like a lost joy – in some other life – and faded . . . and everything else with it . . .

'Nigeria,' I said.

She turned back towards me again. There was something terribly sad about the way she stood. 'Jude,' – it was almost a whisper. 'Forget what I said just now . . . I just meant . . . Well I'm lonely, I guess . . . and when you meet a really straight guy, you sort of hope that something might work out . . .'

No pride. She must have been desperate, poor woman. She just stood there looking at me. And I thought, I needn't have sold those photos! There she stands ready to give me anything I want! Far more than that bastard paid me. And maybe she's a decent sort, really. Maybe she could have saved me from all this. Well, it's too late now. Anyway I don't want it. I don't want her. She's just a middle-aged nympho . . . but somehow pathetic, dabbing her eyes before the mascara started to run . . .

'It's sweet of you to suggest it, Julia,' I said. 'As a matter of fact, I had thought of taking a trip; but I can't get away yet. I've got things that keep me here . . .'

'Sure. Sure. I know you're busy . . .'

She saw it was no good, started towards the door and, as she came by laid her arm against my shoulder, looking up with that pathetic, tragic face. 'I guess I'm just unlucky,' she said. 'There's been nobody for me . . . I mean who really meant anything since . . . since a long time . . . Well now I guess it's too late . . .'

What could I say. 'I'll write to you in New York – if I can make it.' It was the best I could do to comfort her. But she knew I never would and I knew it too.

'I guess I'd better go. I must look awful.' She clutched me to her and offered her cheek to be kissed. Then, with something like a sob, she hurried through the door.

Everything's going round and round in my head. It throbs. I can hardly see. What shall I do? What can I do? I'm caught. Trapped. I don't know what I want. That woman. She has all the money in the world! Yet I pitied and despised her! Why? Am I so wonderful? She'd have despised me if she knew what I'd done. Maybe. Anyway she's gone. She's the last of them. Greg and the Doc too, they've all gone. I'm alone ... She had pots of money. So have I! That's the joke. What good did it do her? What good is it doing me? Why shouldn't I take what came my way? Why not? I'm not guilty of anything. Father said you should never betray a trust. Find your conscience he said. Or was it the Doc? I can't find it, can't find anything. So smug he looked when he gave me the money. He'd corrupted me. Bought me. That's what he thought. Traitor! I could hear it. And the Doc with his 'Oh, Jude!' like an old woman. Why can't they leave me alone? I don't give a damn. I wish I'd never gone to Israel, never set eyes on the bloody scroll. Who cares? A bit of old parchment and probably faked. Greg said it was. I'll go away. I'll start again. I'll do my 'Images of God'. But I can't – not with that money. Every way I turn. They've got me. There's a jinx on it. I can feel it. 'You've conspired to suppress the truth,' that's what they'll say. Judas! It was fated. They'd have got Him sooner or later, somehow. Why blame me?

May God forgive me, I can't live with this ...

CHAPTER FIFTEEN

The last line was scrawled below the rest. Scrawled in that same red ink that Jude Heddon had used to write the will the Inspector had found on the mantelpiece.

John Colvin put the last sheet down on his desk, almost reverently, and sat staring out of the window. What a dreadful thing! What a waste! What a knot the wretched man had got tied up in! Guilt ruined everything. And everybody had contributed to it – his own father, Doc Ramsay, Father Gregory – all of them, in their different ways, had helped to build it up in him ... And he wasn't guilty! He had played quite a secondary role. That was the paradox. He was just the little man, caught, quite innocently, between the millstones of great forces. Father Gregory, and behind him God knows what influences, they were the conspirators, the real traitors.

Sitting there he thought back over the story. From the moment Greg had asked for the translation back, he'd smelt a rat. Those 'superiors' of his, they hadn't caught on at first, they'd been excited, like Greg, by the priceless discovery, they hadn't seen the implications. But when they did! Then the machine was set in motion. It was just a question of how to lose the thing, how to bury the evidence. If Greg had been a bit more discreet with his uncle, Jude would never have known. He would have expected them to publish in due course, as they had said. He was an honest man – a mere pawn in the game – and they'd driven him to suicide! What a thing to have on one's conscience! Poor chap ...

John Colvin sighed deeply. He blamed himself terribly. He ought to have seen it coming. That was his responsibility, as a Samaritan. After all there had been signs. He remembered those questions of his, 'Is there any purpose in life?' 'What does it mean, the remission of sins?' He ought to have understood a man doesn't ask questions like those unless he's deeply worried ... And he was a neighbour too ... But he'd always seemed such a reasonable, sensible chap ... Just because he'd kept it to himself, it had never occurred to him ... You never knew what was going on inside ... Well, there it was ...

He sighed again and picked up the envelope to put the papers back in it. There was something more inside. He tipped it up. Out fell the three wads of notes! He'd forgotten all about them. They'd been in the story; not real. Now, there they were on his desk.

Not on your life! he said to himself. He may have left me everything. That's strange enough. But not this. He certainly wasn't going to take this. He didn't want to touch them. They were tainted somehow. He stared at them. What was he going to do with them? How could he get rid of them? People would wonder how on earth he came by a sum like this. What a stupid complication to get involved in ... He sat for a long time, thinking.

Then his face cleared. He had an idea. But he must talk it over first ... Talk it over with someone who knew all about it, whom he could speak to in confidence. He riffled back through the papers. Brook Cottage, Westcott, that was the address. He would tell him all the tragic business. He felt sure that a man like the Doc would understand him, help him, see his predicament ... His idea was to make the Samaritans a gift of the money. Conscience money. Because he hadn't seen the thing coming, hadn't even tried to help poor Jude ... But first he'd talk it over. Perhaps the Doctor would have a better idea ... He lifted the telephone receiver and dialled Directory Inquiries.

RICHARD HUGO
FAREWELL TO★RUSSIA

Running desperately. Shouting breathlessly. His voice screaming itself
to soundlessness for want of air: 'Get away from here! Get away from
the water!'

The unthinkable has happened at the Soviet nuclear plant at Sokolskoye.
An accident of such catastrophic ecological and political consequence that a
curtain of silence is drawn ominously over the incident. Major Pyotr Kirov
of the KGB is appointed to extract the truth from the treacherous minefield
of misinformation and intrigue and to obtain from the West the technology
essential to prevent further damage. But the vital equipment is under strict
trade embargo . . . .

And in London, George Twist, head of a company which manufactures the
technology, is on the verge of bankruptcy and desperate to win the illegal
contract. Can he deliver on time? Will he survive a frantic smuggling
operation across the frozen wastes of Finland? Can he wrongfoot the
authorities . . . and his own conscience?

'Immensely well-researched . . . growls with suspense . . . even without
the recent memories of Chernobyl the novel has an authentic ring'
Independent

'Diverse loyalties are suspensefully stretched and nerve ends twanged'
Guardian

0 7474 0061 X   THRILLER   £3.50